Praise for
Discovery In Time

Just as readers flocked to Iowa's Madison County in search of R.J. Waller's covered bridges, visitors to Georgia's Thomas County will go hunting for the nesting and resting places of one of this novel's central characters. Written by the region's most sensitive romantic, this tale of ancestral ghosts and a sleepy Southern town will capture the hearts and souls of women who still remember the intensity of their first loves. Who can let such bygones stay forever buried in time? Litherland's novel will bring them to life in all their former glory.

—Jayleen Woods
Editor Emeritus
Florida Hotel & Motel Journal

I've read many stories that fascinate and charm, but rarely do I find one that lives and breathes with such believable suspense. To merely hold my reader's curiosity is never enough, but to grip my heart with honest enchantment is a true joy.

—Arthur L. Zapel
Executive Editor/Publisher
Meriwether Publishing Ltd.

Discovery In Time

Janet Litherland

Cover Art and Illustrations by Bob Dixon

PublishAmerica

Baltimore

First printing

ISBN: 1-59286-373-6

PUBLISHED BY PUBLISHAMERICA BOOK PUBLISHERS

www.publishamerica.com

Baltimore

Printed in the United States of America

Andrea's House

Bob Dixon

Thomasville, Georgia: 1892

Dear Evelyn,
I found out what it is that married people do when they're alone in the bedroom. Remember when we whispered about it in my room back home in London? About the thing that ladies aren't supposed to like? Well, I liked it very much, and now I feel bad because I must be a terrible person!
Aunt Violet told me that is what makes babies. And, Evelyn, I am going to have a baby. I am very frightened! When I told my parents, Mother fell onto the sofa in a swoon, and Father's face turned deep red. I thought he would explode! Actually, he did. Oh, Evelyn, I wish you were here to talk with. I feel so alone! Of course I can talk with Aunt Violet and Becca, but they're adults and it is not the same. Becca comes from a different culture altogether. She said that on the plantation this happens all the time, so she cannot possibly know how I feel. Oh, Evelyn, what will become of me? ...

Thomasville, Georgia: 2002

Chapter 1: *Andrea*

The window was closed; no air moved in the room ... yet the lace curtain at the window fluttered each time Andrea brushed against the polished wood of the old four-poster bed. Same thing had happened several days before. Carefully, she embraced one of the posts and gently stroked the carved pineapple at its top, still watching the curtain. It moved again, almost imperceptibly, but it did move. She wasn't really afraid of ghosts, if that's what this was, especially not this one who'd caused no trouble at all, even seemed friendly. But she did feel some anxiety. And curiosity.

When she and her husband, Alex Ferris, had bought the old Victorian home several months before, the bed came with it. They were told it had been in the house for more than seventy-five years and remained there, because those who were superstitious—meaning nearly everyone in that small South Georgia town—said that bad luck would surely visit whoever had the temerity to remove it.

Andrea sat on the bed. *She* certainly wasn't going to remove it. Such a beautiful piece of furniture! But why had this particular bed received royal treatment over the years? *What makes it special?* she wondered. *The wood? The design? A memory?* ... Gently, she slid her hand up the post once more. She thought she saw a slight movement at the window, but she couldn't be sure.

"Who are you?" she whispered. "Did you live here? Did you sleep in this bed?" She watched the curtain, but nothing happened. "Was that you downstairs in the kitchen yesterday, as I sat at the bar?" she asked aloud. "You know, an entirely different kitchen crossed my line of vision in a blink—different, yet the same. Older. No electric range; no bar. I felt as if I were there, a part of it, at home. Was that your kitchen? ... I can't recall the details of that older room, though I've tried and tried. Like the flash of a camera, it was there and then it wasn't...."

She sighed, feeling and seeing nothing. The "presence" had chosen to remain aloof.

Reluctantly, Andrea left the room and went downstairs to the front porch. The sweet scent of magnolias no longer hung in the air; the gardenias were long gone. It was fall in Thomasville, scorching hot, and Andrea was lonely—alone with illogical visions and happenings that she couldn't capture, identify or explain. Never in her life had she had these kinds of experiences. She wished she had a friend to share them with. How could she talk about ghosts and *déjà vu* with strangers? They'd think she was crazy for sure!

She leaned against the porch railing, remembering the moment she'd first stepped through the front door of the big home she and Alex now owned. First in a long time, that is. That's when it all started. The house had been in Andrea's family for several generations, but after her great-grandmother Cooper had died, none of the remaining family wanted to live in it. Three sets of tenants had rented it over the years, and, for the most part, it had been well kept. Until she and her husband had decided to check it out—one evening during last year's Christmas season—Andrea hadn't been inside the old homestead for nearly thirty years. But the kitchen she had seen briefly in her mind yesterday was not her great-grandmother's kitchen, the one she had visited as a child. It was much older than that.

And what she had experienced that previous Christmas was more than just coming home to her great-grandmother's house. There were flashes of recognition, brief sensations of comfort unrelated to anything in her great-grandmother's time. It was an uneasy kind of peace. And it stuck to her like static electricity.

~~~

Andrea felt perspiration beading on her skin. She walked the length of the front porch and back again, picking at her damp shirt. Despite the heat, she shivered, then closed her eyes against now-familiar and unwelcome thoughts that were pushing themselves into her mind. In addition to the strange sensations often accompanying them, "things" had been gnawing at her, *old* things. She wondered why they should surface now, when life was supposed to be perfect? Alex would be going away for a week, leaving her in this new environment, without friends. *No, that's not it,* she thought. *Memories are making me miserable, painful memories … guilt.* There were lots of things she'd never told Alex in the eight years they'd been married, and she felt guilty for not telling him. How long could she keep it all inside herself?

She shook her head to dissipate the mental cobwebs. There was too much to lose. There was Alex … and he was everything to her, though she'd treated him very badly in the last several days.

Rain began to fall in a light mist. Andrea tucked her short auburn hair behind her ears and moved toward the big front door. Faint sunlight, poking through the misty rain, sparkled on the stained-glass panels on either side. *I'm supposed to be an artist,* she thought, looking at the beautiful panels. *So why can't I get to work? Am I afraid of failure?* Now that she finally had the time and the means, she found it difficult to get started on the only thing she'd wanted to do—to *become*—since childhood; that is, to develop her artistic talent and have a showing in a real gallery. Her mother had scoffed at the idea.

"That's childish nonsense, Andrea," her mother had said. "You've been reading too many magazines. Just because you can draw nice pictures doesn't mean you're one of *them*—an artist. We're a working family. Farmers. You think artists, musicians, movie people and the like live glamorous lives; well, they don't have it so good. It's all puffery! And sinful, too. Put your feet down on the ground where they belong."

Shaking off unhappy memories of her mother, Andrea went inside, hoping for inspiration. She started up the wide staircase, then quickened her pace, heading for the small front bedroom-turned-studio where, it was said, Great-Grandma Cooper had died. When she reached the landing, however, she stopped abruptly. The strangely placed attic door on the next level caught her eye and her imagination, as it did every time she went upstairs. She had never been in the attic.

"It's dangerous," Alex had warned. "Parts of the floor are missing, and there's some old junk up there, probably been there for decades, judging by the dust. It would be easy to lose your footing and take a nasty fall."

But a rainy day is made for exploring, she told herself, continuing up the stairs, slowly now. She paused in the big square upstairs hallway—"hallroom," she had jokingly called it, since it was large enough to be furnished. They had put a rolltop desk in one corner and a floor lamp and love seat along the overhanging banister. A large floor-basket of potpourri made the area smell of apples and cinnamon. On her left was the attic door, beautifully polished, with an ornate brass knob. It was set into the wall a good three feet off the floor. Beneath it, bookcases were built into the wall and filled with Alex's collections of Higgins and Clancy. She had seen Alex go up to the attic on the day they'd completed the purchase of the house. He had opened the door, removed a narrow, four-step stool from the opening, and used it to reach the bottom of the attic stairs.

Now, Andrea hesitated only a second. She turned the doorknob and pulled, exposing a dark, rough stairway of only a few steps that seemed to lead straight into a brick wall! Quickly, she removed the stool and climbed up to the first step, reaching for the long string above her head. With light from the solitary bulb, she could now see more steps, four turning to each side. Carefully, she stepped onto the landing. The steps on her left led to an open room over the back of the house. It had no floor at all, only beams and prickly insulation. And dust. It was dark and gloomy. She pulled a tissue out of her jeans pocket and stifled a sneeze.

Turning right and moving carefully, she stepped up into the other room, the one that faced the street. It was high-ceilinged and much brighter, because the windows at the front of the house were larger. They were also very beautiful—a big picture window in the center, nearly floor-to-ceiling, flanked by two smaller ones. They reminded her of those in her mother-in-law's living room, a "look but don't touch" kind of living room. Her own mother's house had been plain and cheaply furnished, and, as a child, Andrea could touch anything she wanted to except the cookie jar.

"Remember, God is always watching you," Doris had said, more times than Andrea could count. It was impossible to sneak a cookie when God was watching!

Here, however, were these beautiful Palladian windows, wasted in a dust-laden, cobwebby attic. From the outside, Andrea had assumed they were decorative, had no other purpose than to make the façade beautiful. Now she wasn't so sure. The inside framing was lovely, as if intended to grace a room used for living, not just storage. Fleetingly, she sensed having been there before. The image was gone as quickly as it had come. What was it? Sometimes the flashing images made her want to scream in frustration!

She looked up. Overhead, the exposed beams were actually pretty, and the boards of the walls, darkened by nature and dirt over decades of time, were laid in a diagonal pattern. The artist in her responded at once to this unusual beauty, and she was suddenly struck with an idea. *With a little money and a lot of work*, she thought, *this could be a spectacular studio*! She smiled at the possibilities … and realized it was the first time she had smiled in several days. *Really* smiled.

Cautiously, she stepped onto the wooden floor. It was mostly intact, though a few boards were missing. Alex was right. Sure was a lot of junk. A bed frame, a hideous chest of drawers, an old baby carriage.… She stopped, steadying herself against the carriage. *That memory never goes away, does it? Twenty-two years and it still hurts.*

"It doesn't matter, Andrea," Alex had said eight years ago. "It doesn't matter that you can't have children. We don't need a baby to 'make our lives complete,' as you say. My life is complete with you. I love you."

She knew he meant it. Alex Ferris was the sweetest, most wonderful thing ever to happen in her life, and telling him that she could never have his baby was the hardest thing she had ever done. When he said it didn't matter, she wept in his arms, ridding herself of years of unshed tears. It felt good—very good—because she hadn't been able to cry since that terrible night, twenty-two years before, when *it* had happened. She had pushed the whole thing into the deepest pits of her mind and got on with life. There was nothing else she could do if she wanted to survive emotionally. And she did want to survive. More than that, she wanted to win!

She sighed. Her fortieth birthday was just a few months away— a milestone. "The older you get, the tougher you get," her mother had said years before. "Look at me. I had to be tough. Forty-two years old I was when you were born." Though Doris had never said it, Andrea knew that her birth had been a "mistake," that her parents, who married late in life, had not planned to have children.

Being "tough" was one thing Doris had been right about. But when she'd said that Andrea would never get married, that no one would ever want her, she'd been dead wrong. Doris had a mean streak and Andrea cringed at the memory. No tears. She hadn't felt tears on her face for a long, long time. There'd been no time to think about things that made her weep. In her almost-forty years, Andrea Cooper Ferris had done a lot of high-powered climbing and dealing, and it hadn't been easy. She had fought hard for a career she did not want, just to salve the pain and absolve the guilt heaped on her all those years before.

"You've finally done something good," her mother had said, when Andrea had achieved success. "Finally, after dragging the family name through the dirt; God knows how I've suffered!" Andrea didn't cry then, nor since.

She pushed herself away from the dusty old baby carriage and climbed over a box of broken dishes. As she straightened, she noticed something unusual across the room. There was a pole, no, a railing … no, a *bar* fastened along the length of the wall on her right. Carefully, she stepped over a missing floorboard and moved to the bar. She could hardly believe her eyes. It was a *ballet* bar, and it had to be a hundred or more years old, as old as the house itself! She could tell, because there was nothing modern about its design or material, or the way it was fastened to the wall with old-fashioned brass hardware, tarnished and dirty. She touched it, leaving fingerprints in the dust. Then, with sudden inspiration, she put her hand on it and slowly bent her knees outward, as she'd seen ballerinas do on television. She smiled again, lowering her shoulders and stretching her neck high. It felt funny, and she couldn't help giggling aloud. Dancing was neither her talent nor her desire. *But it was to someone*, she thought, *right here in this room.*

She stepped back, her imagination whirling. Did a young Victorian "miss" work out at this bar in her pantalettes? Did she dance in secret? Was she a famous ballerina? Who was she?

~~~

"I explored the attic this afternoon," she said to Alex, as they sat side-by-side at the kitchen bar sipping homemade soup. The kitchen was the one room in the house that had been modernized and made convenient by expanding it over what had once been a back porch. Andrea was thankful over and over again for the big beautiful kitchen, because she loved to cook, and this bright cheery room was a pleasure to work in.

Her husband's blue eyes looked at her over the top of his spoon. "It's a wonder you didn't go through a hole in the floor and break your neck. The attic's a death trap."

"I was careful. Alex, the front side is beautiful! It would make a marvelous studio."

He grinned at her. "I knew it! I knew if you saw it you'd want to work up there in that godforsaken hole." He leaned over and kissed her cheek. "You're a nester, darling. There are twelve big rooms in this house, and you want to build your cozy little nest in the attic with the squirrels."

"Squirrels?"

"Umhmm. In the room at the back, the side that was never finished. We've got to get them out before cold weather comes. Yes, cold weather does come to South Georgia."

"Speaking of finished, what do you suppose the front attic was used for in the past?"

He shrugged. "Storage, I guess. It's not much to look at."

"I don't think so. The windows are huge and the tops of them are latticed—excuse me, 'gingerbreaded.'"

Alex chuckled.

"They're not utility windows, Alex. They were put there for the view."

"But the floor is rough and the walls are unfinished," he said.

"By today's standards, yes. But imagine the room a hundred or more years ago—cleaned, polished and furnished. That room was built for living, not storage."

Alex dipped his spoon into the soup and smiled. "You have a delightful imagination."

Andrea pushed his soup away. "I'm not imagining this," she said. "Alex, did you notice the bar on the side wall?"

"May I finish my soup?"

"It's a ballet bar!"

"It's an old railing. May I finish my soup?"

"No, it's not an old railing, and yes, finish your soup," she said, pushing it back to him. "It really is a ballet bar, a very old one. Someone used that attic a long, long time ago as a dance studio, either privately or to give lessons! Isn't that exciting?"

"I'm trembling."

"Alex Ferris," she chided, "you have no romance in your soul."

"Why would I want it there? I have it in plenty of other places," he said, adding a broad wink.

Andrea laughed. "I noticed."

~~~

"Take a radio up there with you," the elderly neighbor said, stretching his small chest over the picket fence. He wasn't much taller than the posts.

"A radio?" Andrea suspected Mr. Pinckney was a little strange, but at least he was friendly.

"Yes. The squirrels hate it." His voice was high-pitched. "Just turn it on loud and leave it for a few days. They'll move out. You'll see."

"Thanks. I'll try it."

As she opened her front door, she glanced back. He was looking askance at her leaf-strewn yard, the yard she thought was "naturally" beautiful. She smiled to herself.

~~~

Andrea made many trips to the attic during Alex's absence the following week. Each time she returned to the lower floors she carried a huge plastic bag stuffed with trash. After the last trip, all that was left was the baby carriage, which she couldn't handle by herself, and the ugly dresser, which she managed to push and pull into a corner. Storage for art supplies.

She'd also filled a medium-sized carton with items to be donated to Goodwill, disappointed that she hadn't discovered any antiques or good vintage clothing, not even a nice old picture frame. Not one treasure! If anything of interest or value had remained from decades gone by, previous owners or tenants had looted it before Andrea had a chance. Of course there was that four-poster bed in the guest room. It had been in the house during Great-Grandma Cooper's time, except then it was in the small bedroom up front, the room that was now Andrea's temporary studio.

Hands on hips, she surveyed the attic room with satisfaction. It would make a great studio! So what if she didn't find an attic treasure. She had the bed, and the attic room was a treasure in itself. It was meant to be. She knew it was meant to be!

She and Alex, like many successful people who have reached forty-something, were aware that their success was shallow. Both wanted something more—or less. They wanted a slower pace, time to pursue their interests—his in reading, hers in art—and, mostly, more time together. When they finally made the decision to "downshift," they had chosen this house; now, however, Andrea considered that maybe the house had chosen them. That first night they visited, during the annual "Victorian Christmas," the sidewalks of Dawson Street had been lined with luminaries. There were strolling musicians, roasted chestnuts, ladies in long dresses and vintage hats, dapper gentlemen with walking sticks, and horse-drawn carriages clip-clopping up and down Broad Street, still brick-lined after more than a century.

Andrea knew as soon as she had seen the familiar old homestead with welcoming lights in the windows that it was right for them. The tenants, who had already given notice they were moving after the first of the year, had decorated it beautifully.

Inside, the enchantment had escalated—good smells of cranberry mull and hot pumpkin bread, and garlands of evergreen along the staircase and across the overhead latticework in the hall. High ceilings (she loved them because she and Alex were both tall), large rooms, intricate molding, hardwood floors—she had savored the Christmas tour, lagging behind the other visitors, lingering particularly in one of the upstairs bedrooms, where a window curtain fluttered briefly, though the window was closed. *Yes, the curtain!* She had stood very still for a moment, then turned away, hurrying to rejoin the group.

They were in the downstairs parlor, and Alex was warming himself by a low-burning fire. Andrea had sighed. Purred, really, like a kitten.

Alex had put his arm around her. "Nice, isn't it?"

"It's more than nice. It's exactly what we've been looking for."

"Well, for the better part of our last three vacations we've been inspecting houses. We both like this town. We like the house. Why don't we see if your aunt will sell it to us?"

So they had asked. And the widowed aunt who'd owned it, who'd always considered it a burden, was finally able to pay off her debts and move to the apartment complex where her friends were enjoying their last years playing bridge and having tea parties.

Now, as Andrea stood in the center of the cleared and swept space, she felt once again that she had "come home." It was a good feeling, yet anxiety was there too. She shook her head. She'd been in the dust too long and now it was in her brain!

Forcing herself to concentrate on the wide plank flooring, she realized that it wasn't nearly as bad as she first thought. Most of the damage was near the stairway. Only a few odd boards here and there were missing from the main area. Slowly she walked around the room. It was plenty big enough for art equipment. The huge windows were a plus, but she'd still need to install some good lighting. And air-conditioning!

Across the room, she noticed a shiny bit of glass on the floor, something her broom had missed. It was a piece of mirror, very old and discolored. Of course! *Ballet people always dance in front of mirrors.* Sure enough, she could see faint lines on the wall where large mirrors had once hung. *Who were you? When did you live here? What were you like?*

She wandered over to the windows and sat cross-legged on the floor. The sill was so low that she could rest her arm comfortably on it and look out over the porch roof at the historic houses on her street. She never tired looking at them, and they were especially interesting from this angle. She loved the tall, skinny "Half House," built from a Sears Roebuck kit in the 1930s, according to Mr. Pinckney.

"It's called that," he had told her, "because the other half was never built!" Right now, the Half House was empty and for sale.

She sat there, watching and thinking and dreaming for quite a while, until her growling stomach reminded her it was way past lunch time. With effort, because her muscles had grown a little stiff in that position, she pushed herself to her knees. As she did so, a short floorboard next to the window rocked to one side, throwing her off balance, and she toppled over.

"Damn!" she cried, rubbing her skinned knee. "Alex was right. The place is a death trap!"

Because the board was loose and dangerous, she pulled it out and put it aside to be repaired. It was then that she noticed three thick, velvet-bound books in the exposed space. They were stuffed with papers and pictures, and a tintype had fallen from one and lay against it. Stunned, Andrea sat down and carefully lifted the books out through the opening, one by one. They were fragile, a faded pink, and as she held them in her lap, they seemed to come alive with familiarity, though that was impossible, she told herself. Rather, they felt … comfortable … or comforting.

They were diaries, beginning in London, England, January 1892.

> *Dear Diary,*
> *My name is Jenny Alcott, and I love Tyler Fleming almost*
> *as much as I love to dance….*

Andrea had found her treasure.

She held the diaries gently, tenderly, a tiny smile on her face. *I knew it!* she thought. *I was meant to find these books!* She settled back, leaning against the attic windowsill, and began to read.

Chapter 2: *Jenny*

… I love Tyler Fleming almost as much as I love to dance.
And, Dear Diary, he loves me too … At least I hope he does!…

Jenny Alcott had just turned sixteen years old when she fell in love, and it happened rather quickly, taking her very much by surprise. Her mind was on the London stage show she had just seen, on Loie Fuller's spectacular dances—the Fire Dance, the Serpentine, the Rainbow, and the Basket—not on the young man who was trying desperately to get her attention.

"Lovely performance, wasn't it?" he said.

She heard the comment but didn't turn around, not realizing at first that it was directed to her. Her preoccupation was so intense that she had no idea anyone was looking at her, never mind staring.

The evening had been special, not just because of the performance, but because she had been allowed to attend. Though her parents had always spoiled her with money, gifts and lavish clothes, lately they had restricted her social life so completely that it was almost nonexistent! She knew why. It was the curves—they'd popped out of her body in all the right places almost overnight! She stood a little taller and smiled inwardly, recalling her mother's caution.

"Remember, you are maturing in the 1890s, Jenny. London has many temptations to lure an impressionable young woman, especially

20

an inexperienced one from a genteel family. This is a modern city."
Her mother pronounced "modern" as if it were a dirty word.

Even so, Jenny didn't mind. Not really. She had fallen in love
with ballet, dreaming that someday she would become a famous
ballerina. There was no time to think about young gentlemen.

"You've honestly never been *kissed*?" her best friend, Evelyn,
had asked just the day before, as they were looking through fashion
plates in Jenny's spacious bedroom. Evelyn knew *everything*, and
Jenny's parents would have died if they had known *that*! Evelyn was
from such a good family.

"Kissing is absolutely marvelous, Jenny," Evelyn said. "It makes
you feel all squishy inside."

"I can't believe that *squishy* is a good feeling," Jenny replied.

Evelyn giggled. "Of course it is. It's even better when the fellow
brushes up against your body." She lowered her voice. "Especially
your breasts."

Jenny rolled her eyes heavenward. "Breasts are a bother. They
get in the way when I'm dancing." She cupped her hands under her
own tiny ones. "If they get any bigger, I shall have to strap them
down. I don't think I like breasts."

Evelyn's laughter rippled through the air. "Jenny, dear," she said,
trying to sound adult, "the only girls who don't like breasts are girls
who don't *have* them. Yours are *marvelous*." Evelyn loved to say
marvelous. "Just wait until some fellow touches one. You will simply
die, it is so heavenly."

And now Jenny was standing on the *promenoir* at The Empire
Theatre, waiting for the famous Loie Fuller to appear for autographs.
She, her Aunt Violet, Evelyn (who wanted to be called "Eve," for
heaven's sake!), and others had been waiting quite a spell. The air
was a little stuffy, and Jenny's patent-leather slippers were feeling a
bit tight beneath her gown. It was worth it, though, just to see Loie
Fuller up close. Not only that, The Empire was a sight in itself, with
its broad stairways, its chandeliers cascading their light, and its
turquoise and gilt auditorium. Jenny had been there only three times
in her life. She loved watching the elegantly gowned, coiffed and

bejeweled women who strolled the *promenoir*. Everywhere was the rustle of fabric—silk, taffeta, voile and velvet in a rainbow of colors. Even the maiden ladies in plain gowns and lace caps who took people to their seats and sold programs fascinated her.

This evening the crowd was quite moderate, not at all what she had anticipated; nevertheless, a young man was standing very close, much closer than was proper. *Where in the world has Evelyn gone?* she wondered.

"Lovely performance, wasn't it?" He spoke directly to Jenny—she could not miss it this time—the same voice and same words she had heard a moment ago.

She turned slightly toward him, not sure what to do. They had not been introduced. Avoiding his eyes, she mumbled, "Yes, it was lovely."

After a moment he asked, "Do you come here often?"

"Quite often," she lied. She pretended to read her program, effecting the unobtrusive reserve she had noticed in other young women. Where was that Evelyn anyway? And where was Aunt Violet?

Just then someone jostled her from behind and she lost her balance. The young man grasped her arms to steady her. "I say, are you all right?" he asked.

It was then that she looked up at him for the first time. His eyes were dark and snapping with energy, his hair black and curly, even though he'd tried to tame it. He was clean-shaven, and his smile was … well, it was *marvelous*! And he still had not let go of her arms.

"I-I'm quite all right," she stammered.

"Fortunate I was here," he said.

"Yes … yes, thank you."

"Since there is no one to introduce us, I am Tyler Fleming," he offered, releasing his grip and tipping his head slightly.

"Oh," she replied, still overcome by his extraordinary face. Then she noticed his clothes. He certainly was not dressed to attend the theatre—no frock coat or cummerbund. Not even a vest. He had on day clothes, rumpled ones at that.

"And yours?" he asked.

"Wh-what?"

"Your name."

"Uh … Jenny," she answered, recovering. "Jenny Alcott."

"Well, Miss Jenny Alcott, I am happy to make your acquaintance. And please excuse my appearance. I am dressed for work. Here at the theatre, on the Loie Fuller show," he added hastily.

Jenny blinked with new interest. She'd never met a real theatre person. "You … you work with Loie Fuller?"

"Yes. Well, actually, my work on this show is finished. I assisted the designer and supervised construction of the set—the scenery. Now I hang about in case I'm needed for a quick repair."

"Oooh! … I mean, how nice."

"I don't generally come out here after the show," he said, looking around at the crowd, "but I thought I spotted an old friend in the audience. Can't see him now."

"Jenny, dear." The gentle voice at her side belonged to Aunt Violet, her father's younger unmarried sister, who served as Jenny's companion and chaperone in exchange for a home. Jenny adored her.

"Aunt Violet, this is, uh … Mr. Tyler Fleming. He is employed by the theatre company, and he saved me from what might have been a very bad fall. … Mr. Fleming, Miss Violet Alcott, my aunt."

They exchanged pleasantries. "I am not employed directly by the theatre company," Tyler Fleming explained. "I work for the stage designer, who works for himself. We design and build scenery for all types of theatrical productions."

Jenny was impressed, and so was Evelyn when she appeared and demanded to be introduced. Evelyn was so forward! She even told Mr. Fleming that Jenny Alcott was a ballerina, of all things!

"Not really," Jenny said quickly. "I am only a student."

"And with whom do you study, Miss Alcott?" he asked.

"Madame Dupré, on Montague Place."

"In that case, my dear Miss Alcott, you are not 'only' a student. You are an aspiring ballerina. I happen to know Madame Dupré. She accepts no one without genuine talent."

"See, what did I tell you!" Evelyn exclaimed, batting her eyelashes and shaking her blond curls. She was absolutely gushing.

On the way home, as the hansom bumped along the cobblestone streets, Evelyn whispered, "He's really marvelous, Jenny. That's the kind of man I'd love to have touch my breasts."

"Oh, Evelyn!" Jenny whispered back. "Will you please stop talking about *breasts*!"

Aunt Violet smiled into her glove and pretended she hadn't heard.

~~~

Jenny thought about Tyler Fleming all night and all the next day, as she worked out at the ballet bar her father had installed in one of the unused downstairs rooms of their London mansion. She had pestered her parents until they'd agreed to let her "amuse herself" with lessons. They indulged her because they loved her, but they refused to take seriously her passion for dance. The idea of their daughter's becoming a ballerina—a "theatre person"—was too ridiculous to consider. And they were not the least bit interested in the stage antics of Loie Fuller!

Jenny held onto the bar, stretching and bending her body from one position to another ... and thought about Tyler Fleming's eyes. They were so ... so alert. Even as she had turned to go last night, his eyes never left her. She could feel them burning into her back as she walked away.

Jeté, jeté, sauté, plié—she pirouetted around the room, wondering what excuse she could possibly use to attend the same show twice.

Mr. Fleming, however, was one step ahead of her. He was outside Madame Dupré's studio when Jenny emerged from her lesson the following Thursday. Aunt Violet, of course, was with her.

"Well," he said. "Fancy meeting you here! I was just going in to confer with Madame Dupré."

He was lying and Jenny knew it. His laughing eyes betrayed him. He had contrived to meet her again, and she was thrilled!

Tyler tugged at his watch fob and said, "Since I am a bit early, may I treat you ladies to a cup of tea?" He indicated the tea and sweet shop next door.

Jenny smiled and pleaded silently with Aunt Violet, who replied, "A cup of tea would be lovely, Mr. Fleming."

~~~

"I know!" said Evelyn, suddenly coming up with an idea. "Give a party! Invite some of your classmates at Madame Dupré's, and me of course, and that dreadful Angus Newton because that would keep your parents happy, and that brother and sister who live on Bruton Street off Berkley Square—your mother likes their mother. Anyway, include Tyler Fleming on the list. You must provide an opportunity for your parents to meet him, Jenny. Otherwise, things will never progress."

"Things?"

Evelyn giggled. And they planned a *marvelous* party.

~~~

Jenny's mother liked the idea, though she had no inkling of her daughter's motive and never questioned the guest list, except to add a few names. Jenny hoped the excitement wouldn't bring on one of her mother's "spells" and spoil the party. Millicent's spells were fairly frequent and seemed at times to be oddly convenient.

"The party will be in the ballroom," her mother said, "and of course we'll want to include several adult couples to help chaperone."

"Of course," Jenny replied dutifully.

"We will all be dancing and enjoying ourselves, dear," Millicent said. "Your young friends won't even notice us."

Jenny doubted that.

~~~

She learned a lot about Tyler Fleming at the party. She learned that his parents were not wealthy, but neither were they poor. With hard work they had managed to send him to Oxford, where he had read architecture; and they were disappointed that he had chosen to build theatrical scenery instead of houses.

"Couldn't help it," he said. "I like being around the theatre. It excites me, and I have a talent for the work." Suddenly he whispered in her ear, "You excite me, too, Jenny."

She gasped.

"Oh, don't be shocked," he said. "You feel it too. I know you do. You've excited me from the moment I saw you at the theatre, standing there on the *promenoir*, exquisitely lovely and enraptured by the evening's experience. What a vision you were ... you *are*." He pulled her onto the dance floor, and their bodies touched momentarily. Jenny's skin tingled with pleasure, and she blushed. She hoped he wouldn't notice.

Very properly, Tyler held her away from him as they danced. And, very properly, he held his head high and his mouth stiff, as if he were sucking a pickle. But his eyes were twinkling, and Jenny laughed. He was a wonderful dancer, and in that moment she was sure she was in love, whatever that meant. She could think of nothing else. It was a *marvelous* feeling!

A little later, while Tyler was dancing with Evelyn, Jenny's mother pulled her aside. "You're spending entirely too much time with that one young man, dear. Do I know him? Who is he?"

"Oh, a ... a friend of Madame Dupré," she replied, feeling a bit guilty.

"Surely he's not a theatrical dancer?"

"No, he's an architect." It was the truth, Jenny decided quickly, if not the whole truth. "His name is Tyler Fleming."

"Of the Bedford Square Flemings?" her mother asked with a hopeful smile.

"I'm not sure."

"Well, pay more attention to your other guests. Poor Angus looks lonely."

"Poor Angus" was the horse-faced snob that Barclay and Millicent

Alcott had chosen as a husband for their only daughter. His mouth *always* held an imaginary pickle! But his family was rich and titled, and he was besotted with Jenny. *Not in a million years*, Jenny thought, *will I marry that man, titled or not*!

"Yes, Mother," she answered.

Later, Jenny and Tyler stepped outside for some air. Mr. and Mrs. St. John were positioned to chaperone from the veranda, but they were so engrossed in their own conversation that they did not notice two young people slipping into the shadows.

Tyler took Jenny into his arms immediately and kissed her, and she didn't hesitate to kiss him back. It was the most wonderful thing that had ever happened to her! Evelyn was right! He kissed her eyelids, too, and her hair, and he held her body tightly against his, so that she could feel her breasts pushing into his chest. Oh, God—she was melting inside! She was *squishy*!

"Jenny, I love you," he said. "I can't explain how anything could happen so quickly but it has. I love you, and that's all there is to it."

Jenny was not sure what it involved, loving a man, but she was sure that she never wanted to let go of this one. "I love you, too, Tyler," she whispered.

As he crushed his mouth onto hers once again, he groaned. He actually did. She heard him!

"Before I leave tonight," he said, "I am going to ask your father if I may call on you. We are going to do this right, my darling, because I do not want to chance losing you."

Jenny was overcome with emotion. She was so lucky. Tyler was wonderful. How could her father possibly refuse a proper request from one who was so obviously a gentleman?

~~~

"You want *what*?" her father thundered at them in his study. "Young man, we do not even know you. Besides, my daughter has been promised to someone else, albeit a few years away."

"By you, Father, not by me," Jenny replied quietly. "I do not even like Angus Newton, let alone love him."

"You can learn to love him, bygod! Just as I learned to love your mother. It's a suitable match."

Jenny fled the room in tears.

~~~

For the next two months Jenny was morose and uncommunicative. The only thing she showed any interest in was her ballet class with Madame Dupré, for it was there that she met Tyler each week after her lesson for a cup of tea at the nearby shop. Always with Aunt Violet, naturally. And each week Aunt Violet would excuse herself to look at the molasses candies and other sweets for sale in the case, so that the young couple could have a few moments alone.

"Aunt Violet," Jenny confided one evening in her aunt's sitting room, "I could not bear life without seeing Tyler, and I could not manage even *that* without your help. You cannot possibly know how much I appreciate it."

"Oh yes, I can, my dear." Violet patted Jenny's knee as they sat side by side on the pretty Duncan Phyfe sofa. "Once, a long time ago, I was faced with a similar kind of dilemma. I loved a delightful young tradesman, whom my father—your grandfather—considered 'inappropriate.' I did not have your spunk and spirit, Jenny dear, and propriety was so ingrained in young women of my day that I could do no less than respect my father's wishes."

"Which were?"

"He kept me in the house for several weeks, then told me I was 'free,' but that I must never see my young man again."

"Did you? See him, I mean?"

"No, dear … I never saw Samuel again."

Jenny couldn't believe her ears. She had never thought about Violet that way, her being interested in a young man, that is. Now she felt extremely selfish that she had never asked, though her mother would have called it "prying." If she had thought about it at all, she would have supposed that Aunt Violet had chosen to be an old maid.

But now she looked closely at the woman beside her. Why wouldn't she have been interested in men? This was a beautiful person, still stylishly attractive, though nearly thirty years old, and kind, thoughtful ... she would have been a wonderful wife.

"You didn't see him again, even once?" Jenny asked.

Violet shook her head. "Not once."

Jenny felt a sudden rush of love for her aunt. "I didn't know," she said, taking the older woman's hands in her own.

"Of course you didn't. We do not talk of such things in polite society," Violet answered with a wry smile. "But I did have enough spirit to refuse to marry the man my father had chosen." She sighed, and her face took on a pensive look. "That, too, was probably a mistake, because my life has been a lonely one, especially now, as I'm growing older. Oh, I have you, dear, and your family," she added quickly. "But it's ... it's not quite the same. I have spent many sorrowful hours aching with regret that I'd walked away from my Samuel." Her eyes filled with tears. "I don't want that to happen to you, Jenny. I want you to have, at the very least, the opportunity to make a choice."

Jenny threw her arms around her aunt and wept.

Chapter 3: *Alex*

Alex was propped up in bed in his room at New York's Palace Hotel, trying to concentrate on the *Wall Street Journal*. He'd never stayed in this monstrous building—too ostentatious for his taste—but his favorite little neighborhood hotel was booked full, and the Palace was hosting the conference. He could work, eat and sleep in the same building. Wouldn't have to be out in that nerve-jangling Manhattan traffic at all. That suited him fine. More and more he dreaded anything that smacked of activity, anything that would take him out of the quiet, slow pace of South Georgia, away from Andrea. Especially away from Andrea.

Last week, though, she'd scared the hell out of him when she said she didn't want to sit and watch the world go by.

"What does that mean?" he'd asked.

"I don't know, Alex." She looked away, but not before he saw tears forming. He'd never seen her cry, and suddenly there was a terrible wrenching deep within him. He sat down on the edge of a fragile old love seat, while Andrea paced. They were in the front parlor, the one room in the house where he'd never felt at ease.

"I thought you wanted to make this move," he said. "I thought you liked Thomasville."

"I did. I *do*. It's just … I don't know. I'm having a hard time with all this … this quietness!" She slammed her hand down on the keys of the grand piano, making a god-awful racket. Alex jumped up. She said, "I feel like I need to get dressed up and go to an office somewhere. See some people. Do something important!"

He'd known something was bothering her, and he knew they ought to talk about it, but he'd kept putting it off, hoping that whatever it was would go away so that Andrea could focus on her art, and he could stop feeling like the villain in a play he didn't understand.

"Come sit beside me," he said, starting back to the love seat. Then, thinking better of it, he took her hand. "Let's go to the den before you break something in here." He noticed the tiniest upturn at the corner of her mouth, kissed it quickly, and led her to the big, comfortable sofa on the other side of the foyer.

He was pretty sure the problem was a simple matter of adjustment to a new way of life, to a city totally different from Atlanta. They hadn't been here long enough yet to have any real friends, and they hadn't found much to do together, other than fixing up their house.

"You've always wanted time to paint," he said, once they were seated. He held her hands. "This is supposed to be your chance to chase a dream."

"I know," she replied, holding her head high. No sign of tears now. "But maybe that's all it is, a dream, a childhood fantasy."

"That's ridiculous. Everyone has dreams. My grandmother dreamed of going to college one day; and, if you'll remember, she graduated three years before she died. Those were the proudest three years of her life, Andrea. Dreams are achievable."

"But maybe I don't have any talent. Maybe I just thought I did, and the people who complimented me were simply being nice. Maybe the whole idea of being an artist was a romantic whim. Otherwise, why can't I get started? Why can't I get on with it, like you have? You haven't had one bit of trouble adjusting!"

"It's just taking you a little longer. And you *do* have talent. Remember that man and his wife who came to visit when we first moved in? The man who paints those beautiful roses? His paintings hang in museums all across the country, in the White House, even in Buckingham Palace. He knows what's good, and he said *you* were good." Alex pointed across the room. "He looked at the canvasses you had stacked over there at that time and was impressed. Do you remember?"

She nodded. "He was being friendly, something not too many people around here are."

Alex ignored the last part of her comment. "I don't agree." He lifted her fingers to his lips and kissed them. "You have talent. Lots of talent, right here in these hands and fingers."

"It's so hard to do, Alex. It's so hard! All of a sudden I feel old ... and lost."

"You're neither old nor lost, sweetheart," he said, putting his arms around her. "I found you. Remember?"

She managed a smile.

"Sure it's hard to adjust. It's difficult to get started because you're out of practice. So, isn't that the best place to put all your excess energy? Go after your artwork like you'd go after a contract. Think of it as an investment. An investment in your future. *Our* future."

She brightened a little. "I might could do that."

"'Might could'?"

"That's the way I talked, growing up."

Alex chuckled and hugged her tightly to his chest. Andrea had grown up in rural Alabama. That had amazed him at first—that she'd gone from a soybean farm to a brokerage boardroom. Of course he hadn't known then how hard she'd had to work to get there. She handled the business like she'd been born to it. She was the smartest, feistiest, yet most adorable woman he'd ever met—a true enigma— and he'd fallen in love with her so slowly and comfortably that he didn't realize what was happening until his heart was gone forever.

~~~

Now, he put his *Wall Street Journal* aside and thought back through that conversation. She seemed to have lost all her motivation. Lately, she'd been walking through the house as if she were dazed— straightening pictures that weren't crooked, opening and shutting those lacy Victorian curtains as if she couldn't make up her mind. He wished she'd take the damn things down and get something new. When he'd said that to her, she'd glared at him as if he'd just suggested putting sugar on cottage cheese! He'd thrown up his hands and left the house. God, he hated "scenes." He hadn't been raised that way.

Since her phone call last night, though, something had changed. Clearly, she was obsessed with cleaning the attic; and even though he'd rather she stay in the nice little second-floor studio, he knew—he just *knew*—she'd move her studio to the treetops. There was no way in hell he'd discourage her now. Let her renovate the rafters, if that's what it took!

But had their conversation really solved anything? Was he missing something? Sometimes it seemed like she wanted confrontation, questions, but he'd never been a probing sort of person. His folks had taught him always to accept people as they were and to give them lots of space in return. That, in fact, had been one of the things Andrea had said early on that she loved about him, that he'd given her lots of space in their relationship. Did she have too much space now? How the hell could he measure "space"?

He reached for his Perrier on the bedstand, suddenly thirsty. *Maybe it's the baby thing*, he thought. She hadn't said a word about it since that one time, when she told him she couldn't have children. He'd said it didn't matter, and he'd meant it. Andrea was all he needed. But he knew it still bothered her. He could tell the by the way her face changed when one of her friends announced she was pregnant, or when they'd pass a baby carriage in the park, or when she'd see toys in a store window. And especially since they'd moved away from Atlanta and things had quieted down.

He'd never asked why she couldn't have children. Again, it didn't matter. He had the feeling that it was a very touchy subject, so he gave her plenty of that damned "space" with it. He'd always figured that if she wanted to tell him, she would.

He laid his head back on the pillow.

Andrea had warned him on their first date that artistic folk were a strange lot. "We're moody," she had said. "Sometimes introspective, sometimes outspoken. We often follow whims, rather than doing the expected. We're not very logical. I really had to work at that when I went into the investment business—that kind of life takes a stiff mix of whim and logic."

"I like weird people," he'd replied with a smile. But later, when he decided to ask her to marry him, he admitted to himself that her whimsy (like her recent moods) was a little scary—exciting and scary. He sure as hell would never be bored with Andrea Cooper.

Alex sighed. He was all logic. Didn't have an artistic bone in his body. Couldn't really even appreciate the stuff, especially that modern gobbledygook. Thank heaven Andrea painted things he could at least recognize and make an intelligent comment about.

All that talk about following dreams. He couldn't remember ever wishing for anything. He'd always had what he needed and most of what he wanted. His parents were accommodating, but in no way indulgent. They were a real team—disciplined him constantly with love and were always there for him. Still were.

As he thought about his life, he realized that he'd never had to struggle as Andrea had. He'd done everything "right"—been a good student and a high school athlete, had great friends. Girls hadn't been a problem either. Well, except for one. He'd never had trouble getting dates. That one, though. She'd really upset him. And it was his junior prom, of all things. She'd just moved to town, so he didn't know her, but she was the prettiest girl he'd seen in a long time, and she said she'd go with him. He rented a tux, bought a corsage, borrowed his dad's car, and went to pick her up. When he got to her house, there was another car in the drive and another boy in a tux, holding another corsage of the same color. Stephanie—that was her name—came out of the house and took the other boy's arm.

"I decided to go with him," she said to Alex. "Sorry."

Alex's heart nearly stopped beating, and the other boy's face visibly paled. "What?"

She shrugged and opened the car door for herself. The other boy, whom Alex knew slightly, turned to him and apologized. "I didn't know about this, I swear," he said. "I'll walk away right now."

"No, that's okay," Alex said. "Go on and take her."

"I'm not sure I want to."

Alex turned and left, and for a long time after that he had a problem with rejection. Things that ordinarily would have rolled off him like rain over glass began to cling with tough little tentacles, and he became vulnerable. To compensate, he built an invisible shield around himself. He didn't get hurt, but he didn't get involved either. He had lots of friends, but no "special" friends. Then, when he went to college, things turned around. College was a new world with new experiences, new excitement, and it fit him like a sleek diving suit.

The only time he ever again experienced that fear of rejection was when he asked Andrea Cooper to marry him. He was absolutely terrified she'd say no. When he'd put that single red rose in a crystal vase to set the scene, his hand had trembled remembering the pretty corsage he'd tossed into a Dumpster years before. But this time the girl—woman—had said yes.

~~~

Now, away from Andrea, he was feeling vulnerable again. What was *really* bothering her? He wanted to know but hadn't wanted to ask, because he was afraid of getting an answer he didn't want to hear. Just when life was getting to be the best it had ever been. *Well, if screwing things up even worse will make our lives better in the end, that's what I'll do*, he promised himself. *I'll be a royal screw-up—I'll confront her*!

The phone rang. He glanced at his watch. It was 10:30 p.m., and he had talked with Andrea earlier. He answered the phone and smiled as he heard his dad's voice. His folks never went to bed until after the eleven o'clock news. In a few seconds his mom had picked up the extension.

"I'm so glad you gave us this number, Alex," Mrs. Ferris said. "We've missed hearing your voice."

They went through their usual kinds of questions—anything new happening, how are things at the conference, how's the new family law practice coming along, how's Andrea?

"Well, to be honest, she's a little restless."

"That's understandable," Mom said. "I'd be a nervous wreck if I were suddenly uprooted and moved out of Atlanta."

"She wasn't 'uprooted,' Mom. She wanted to move as much as I did; and it wasn't sudden. We'd been planning it for a long time."

"Planning is different from doing," she said.

Dad added, "But she'll settle in, son. Give her time."

"I'm not so sure, Marshall," Mom said to Dad. "I think—"

Then, as he'd done so many times in the past, Alex settled back and listened to them talk it out—never arguing, but never afraid to disagree. And, as usual, they made pretty good sense.

"Tell me something, Alex," Mom said finally. "Have you and Andrea been taking advantage of cultural opportunities since you moved?"

Alex laughed. "Cultural opportunities! Are you kidding?"

"No. I'm not. I've been reading up on your Thomasville. The city is historic, for one thing. Most of the downtown buildings have been restored and look just like they did in the 1800s. Both of you enjoy history. And there's a cultural center that hosts performing arts, plus an art gallery and art exhibitions. Andrea would love that!"

"I, uh, I guess I didn't know that," he answered a little sheepishly.

"There also are big old homes open to the public, including a plantation."

"We *live* in a big old home, Mom."

Mrs. Ferris ignored his comment. "Have you been to so much as a *movie*, Alex?"

"Well—"

"I thought not. There's an excellent drama company, too, according to what I've read, and they have live theater productions. Your father and I went to Agatha's the other night—you remember, right across from The Fox?"

"I haven't forgotten Atlanta, Mom."

"Well, we had the most wonderful time! The actors came right out into the audience to speak their lines!"

Alex could picture the gleam in his mother's eyes as she spoke, and he realized he hadn't seen that gleam in Andrea's eyes for quite a while. No, they hadn't even been to a movie. He'd been content to stay home. Maybe he'd become *too* comfortable with his new life. Too complacent.

"That's a good idea, Mom," he said. "When I get home, I'm going to see to it that Andrea gets out of the house to do something fun. It'll be good for both of us."

When he put the receiver back in its cradle, he felt better, as he always did after talking with his folks, and that amazed him. Here he was, forty-four years old and still able to get a lift from hearing their voices, even when there was nothing much to talk about.

Andrea hadn't been so fortunate. Her father had died when she was a teenager, and her mother just a few years ago. They were quite elderly—more like grandparents than parents—and she'd never been able to talk with either of them. They were good people, but extremely narrow-focused. Not much was open for discussion. What a life she'd had. When he thought about it, Alex wondered how she'd come through it so well, without any scars, at least that he could see.

Of course he didn't discover any of this until he'd known her for a long time. Even then she only doled it out in bits and pieces. They'd been married eight years now, and he was still learning about her. Just last month she told him about seeing her cousin killed by a freight train when they were children.

"I was blamed for it, Alex," she'd said, "because I was seven years old, after all, and he was only four."

"Someone actually told you that you were to blame? For something so horrendous? They said that to a child?" Alex was stunned.

She nodded. "I should have been watching him closer."

"I don't believe this. I mean, I do, but ... a seven-year-old should never have been put in charge of an active four-year-old."

"Well, I was. And I was told that Danny's death was most certainly all my fault." She looked away. "I wasn't permitted to go to the funeral, even though I begged to. I wanted to see Danny one last time, to tell him how sorry I was."

"Andrea, it was not your fault. There should have been an adult watching both of you! The *adults* were at fault."

"I don't want to talk about it anymore," she'd said, walking away.

He'd watched her leave the room. *God, what a family!* he'd thought.

Alex knew she was tough, but she was also fragile. Much as he loved her, he'd never wanted to probe her past. Anything she told him had to be her decision. He'd wanted it that way. But now ... now that she was struggling with something inside of herself ... he would have to change his ways.

~~~

I want to take a gift to her, he thought, *something she'll really like. Maybe several gifts.* So Alex Ferris went shopping for the first time in his life, or at least the first time he could remember. When he was young, his mother shopped for him. Even in high school he asked her to choose gifts for him to give. In college his best friend's girl did the shopping. And in business his assistant made the choices. She had impeccable taste and a good idea of the kinds of gifts he wanted. He never cared what things cost. Never even looked, just paid the bills. Now he was on his own in New York City. What would he buy?

He started with jewelry, because Andrea liked pretty but simple pieces, and he liked seeing them on her. He found a silver brooch in the shape of an artist's palette. The "paint splashes" were made of semi-precious stones—peridot, citrine, blue topaz, garnet and amethyst. Andrea would love it!

In a little shop on Lexington Avenue, he bought a colorful silk scarf encircled with carousel horses, and a tapestry pillow that had been designed from a Wolkins watercolor.

He thought he was finished, but something in the window of an antiques store caught his eye—a silver-plated Victorian picture frame in an intricate floral pattern that Andrea would love! Knowing her, she'd hound the antiques shops until she found an old photograph to put in it. It would give her something to do. Thank heaven there were plenty such shops in Thomasville. That was how they'd managed to furnish their parlor, choosing all the right period pieces. The room now looked authentic, but as far as Alex was concerned, it was stiff as hell. The only piece of furniture in there he really liked was the "square" grand piano that was really rectangular and that neither of them knew how to play.

He picked up his packages and left the store. As he walked, he hummed an old tune, something he hadn't done in a long time. The shopping had been fun.

Alex hadn't wanted to spend an entire week in New York—he'd grumbled about going and leaving Andrea—but now that it was nearly at an end, he had to admit it'd been good for him. He'd had time to think.

Andrea. The love of his life was worth thinking about. Was worth doing something about. Was worth … well, everything.

He slept soundly.

Chapter 4

Andrea brushed her fingers gently across the page. The tears that stained it were more than one hundred years old, yet they seemed as real as if they had been shed yesterday. Jenny had wept for her Aunt Violet's wasted life, and probably some of the tears had been for herself as well.

How did Jenny get from England to this house in America? Andrea wondered. *And why?* She was sure she would find the answer somewhere in the following pages.

Reluctantly, she closed the little book. She had been reading for more than an hour, and daylight was fast fading. She felt weak, as if she had been inside Jenny's skin. There was a knot in her stomach, too, a twisting of empathy, not only for Jenny, but also for Violet. And, though it disheartened her to admit it, even for herself.

The diary was forcing her to remember, to think, and it wasn't easy. Three lives—Jenny's, Violet's and her own—dictated by propriety and tradition. Jenny was young, and she had a warm, loving confidante. At least that counted for something. But Andrea felt particularly sorry for Violet. She hadn't stood a chance. If that forward-thinking woman had lived a century later, she would most certainly have been part of the women's movement. Violet was doing her best for Jenny, but Andrea had an idea that, as she read further in the diaries, she would find that Violet's help wouldn't be enough.

Tradition could be a formidable opponent.

"This is the Deep South, Andrea. The Bible Belt," her mother often had reminded her. "I'm proud to live here, and you should be too."

"But why do we have to care about what other people think of us?" asked the child Andrea.

"We have to show them that we're *good* people. We have to set an example."

The child didn't want to be an example. She just wanted to be a child. Her feelings about her mother ran the gamut. She loved her, but she also feared her, and that fear continued into adulthood. Doris Cooper had that power.

As she grew into adolescence, Andrea learned that "sex" was the dirtiest of words, and *saying* that word was only slightly less terrible than taking the Lord's name in vain. Doris was extremely moralistic, yet seemed to be terrified of her own shadow. This narrow-mindedness and confusion had nearly cost Andrea's life. That was one of the many times when Doris' eyes got that wild look and her voice went up several pitches, times when things didn't go "right," meaning *her* way. If Andrea, after her recovery, hadn't dug into a career with strength and determination—even though it wasn't her *chosen* career—her emotional well-being also might have been at stake.

She never blamed her mother, though, only herself for not being able to measure up. How could she blame a mother who was trying so hard to make up for her own beginnings?

"I was an orphan," Doris often reminded her. "Never knew what it was like to be part of a real family until the Meades adopted me. By then I was a strapping twelve-year-old who could help them on their farm, and help I did! Worked from sunup to sundown, I did, and squeezed my school work in as best I could. You know, some folks' reasons for wanting children have nothing to do with love!"

Andrea still could hear the resentment and bitterness in her mother's voice. She wasn't sure that Doris had ever loved her husband. They were in their late thirties when they married, and

Andrea wasn't born until her mother was forty. Despite that "mistake," they did their best for her.

"You're loved, Andrea Jane, loved and cared for by parents who treat you right and want you to grow up to be a good, God-fearing person."

Truth was, Andrea feared her mother more than she feared God. But how could anyone argue with that kind of logic? Doris had tried, in the only way she knew. With blinders firmly in place, she marched straight ahead doing good. Always doing good.

But then the "terrible thing" happened when Andrea was eighteen, the most terrible thing her mother could ever imagine. Worse, even, than murder.

"It's a good thing your father has gone on to heaven," her mother had said to her, "because you surely would have broken his heart here on earth. Like you've broken mine," she added.

Years later, however, Mother was proud. I made her proud of me!

Well, Andrea's mother was in heaven now, too, and none of it mattered anymore … or did it?

I cannot think about it! She pushed herself to her feet. When the memories came back, so did the old feelings of guilt and shame, and she didn't want to deal with them. She had been pushing them down and stomping on them for twenty-two years.

~~~

Clutching the diaries, Andrea carefully crossed the attic, avoiding the pitfalls. As she had done the previous night, she stopped to turn on her little battery-powered radio before going down the stairs. It was set for loud country music, the whanging kind. She couldn't help laughing at herself just a little for following Mr. Pinckney's advice. Maybe she was as goofy as her neighbor seemed to be.

"Night-night, squirrels," she said, wondering if it really would work.

She stopped in the little front bedroom on the second floor, where she had arranged her art supplies. It was a pretty good studio, a cozy room. Briefly, she wondered if she should be content with it and forget the attic. A movement at the window caught her eye—the curtain fluttered once ... then again, and the window was closed. But the four-poster was not in this room, and that had always been the catalyst. Andrea went over to the curtain and took hold. The fluttering stopped. She looked upward, but the window was tight, no draft. Just then she heard the air-conditioning click on. *That's it*, she thought. *This old house is trying to get used to central air.* Later, she would realize that her logic was faulty.

There was leftover casserole in the refrigerator—a good thing, because she was very hungry, and it would be easy and quick to zap it with microwaves. She was anxious to return to the diaries, even though they dredged up old pain. Andrea wanted to find out what had happened to Jenny, how she had come to live in her house, to dance in her attic. It was exciting, and it was something to do while Alex was gone.

He phoned as she was clearing the dishes.

"Still miss me?" he asked.

"Of course. This big house is lonely, especially at night."

"What about the big bed?"

"That, too." She smiled to herself. Alex was a wonderful lover as well as her best friend. She shouldn't have acted like a miffed child. She would make it up to him when he got home.

"How many trips have you made to the attic?" he asked. "Come on, how many?"

"Uh, six or seven," she admitted. "But I'm almost finished now."

"I knew it! I knew you'd go up there again and again."

"You'll be glad I did. It's clean now. And Alex ... I found something very interesting. I found some diaries, and they're over a hundred years old!"

"You've been reading them."

"Of course I have!" Andrea's excitement sped her words along. "They belonged to a young girl who grew up in London. That's all I know so far, except that she was a dancer and she loved someone her father didn't approve of. Her father had another young man picked

43

out for her. I'm guessing that she came to America and moved into our attic, maybe rented it. That's her ballet bar, of course. Maybe the boy she loved came with her. He was a stage designer—"

"Slow down!" Alex laughed. "You sure you're not reading a dime novel?"

"Where'd you learn that old-fashioned term? Read a few yourself?"

"I miss you. Go on and enjoy. Nose through those old diaries all day tomorrow, because when I come home Saturday night, I want you all to myself."

"Alex, do you believe I'm being nosy?"

"Of course, but who will care after a hundred years?

"Who, indeed? Love you, darling."

She missed him. When she'd met him, he'd been a reluctant partner in a prestigious firm of corporate lawyers, where the other partners were more interested in billable hours than in serving clients. He had come to her for investment advice; and, as his portfolio grew, so did his interest in Andrea Cooper. And hers in him. She was attracted to everything about him, including his thick, silvery hair. He had been a true blonde, gone prematurely gray. Andrea thought his hair looked dashing against his suntanned skin and deep blue eyes. He thought it looked old. It wasn't love at first sight for either of them, but a growing, warming, wonderful kind of enlightenment that one day exploded into passion. She was thirty-two and he was thirty-six, both with busy lives, neither with a particular concern about getting married. But they did. It felt right.

And it had continued to feel right until lately. Until Alex had become so ... so satisfied! Sometimes she felt like smacking him for being able to do what she could not. Alex's downshifting, unlike hers, had been meteoric—all the way to "crawl" in a matter of days. No problem for him. He was content to spend a few hours each day at his small office and the rest of the time with his feet propped up and a book in his hands.

~~~

Alex looked in the mirror, adjusting his tie. She'd sounded wonderful, excited, like the old Andrea, not the tormented one of the last few weeks. He could hardly wait to get home to her and to give her the gifts. Right now, though, he had to get downstairs to meet a couple of guys he'd run into at the conference. One he'd known in law school; the other was a new acquaintance. They were having drinks there in the Palace, then going to Romeo Salta for dinner. Actually, he'd been looking forward to it all day, and that surprised him. He wouldn't have believed that anything smacking of the "old life"—getting dressed for a late dinner, a night out with the guys—would have had any appeal.

He got on the elevator thinking about Andrea and the diaries, smiling to himself. He was glad she'd found them. That was exactly the kind of thing she loved—digging around in the past. When she would pick up a book for pleasure, she'd always choose history or historical novels, then she'd want to visit the sites to see where the action had taken place. She'd spend hours roaming through antique shops, wondering who might have sat on some old broken-down chair, or whose hands had worn the handle thin on a butter churn. She loved Victorian photographs, even had one made of herself all dressed up in a pinched-in gown and feathered hat. Looked damned uncomfortable, if you asked him, but she sure was happy.

He thought of the silver frame he had bought and how much she'd like it, and was so pleased with himself that he actually grinned a wide grin, showing teeth like a Cheshire cat. Suddenly, the woman beside him in the elevator stomped her foot, bringing him back to reality, and Alex realized that he'd been grinning at *her*. She looked as if she wanted to punch him in the nose, and could. Thank God the ride was over!

~~~

The drinks were good, the dinner was good, and the conversation was especially good. He and Doug, his old college buddy, had a lot to catch up on, and Shekhey, the new acquaintance, was from Egypt and had all sorts of interesting tales to tell.

As they were ordering dessert, three very attractive women appeared at their table. Alex was surprised. He'd thought those days were over. After all, he was forty-four now, though he really didn't look it, he thought as he stood, straightening his tie. He started to speak, but Doug was already on his feet making introductions.

"Guys, I'd like you to meet Margo, Renee, and Charlotte." Doug had a devilish smile on his face, and Alex's heart sank. "I asked them to join us for, uh, dessert," Doug added, motioning for three chairs to be brought over.

Alex didn't want this. The women were good-looking, nicely dressed, well-spoken … and, he realized now, well-paid! How could he escape? Not easily, he thought, as they squeezed around the table. He didn't mind offending Doug—they were old friends—but he certainly didn't want to offend Shekhey. Well, he'd get through the *actual* dessert, and then get away. Somehow.

"Uh, just *tortoni* for me," he said, when the waiter returned. He patted his stomach. "Having a little indigestion. Maybe that will settle it." And that gave him The Idea: He was pretty sure he could make himself real sick before it was time for the *other* dessert!

One good thing, he thought, *these women sure don't look like hookers*. They were a real class act. Charlotte was next to him. Her black dress was tasteful, though a trifle low-cut, and her make-up wasn't overdone at all. A little conversation over coffee couldn't hurt anything. But afterward, he had to get away. This sort of thing hadn't been part of his life since Andrea. He didn't want it.

Alex ate very slowly, trying to buy time, trying to figure out what to do, how to fake an illness, how to get Charlotte to move over—she was too close and cuddly. He ate so slowly, in fact, that his *tortoni* became a pale, thin liquid. Looking at that melted mess nearly did make him sick. He made a face at Doug, but Doug was too pleased with himself to realize that Alex wasn't happy. Above all, Alex wasn't happy with Charlotte. What she looked like and what she was were two different things. She'd warmed up in a lot less time than it took his *tortoni* to melt!

"Tell me about your business," she said. Her hand was on his thigh.

"Not much to tell." He shrugged and tightened his tie again.

"Oh, now, I don't believe that. You look like a very interesting person." Her hand crept upward.

"I'm married," he blurted, a little too loudly. But the other four hadn't noticed.

"Well, that's interesting," she said. "Married men have such a wide scope of experience to draw on."

What the *hell* was she talking about? He picked up his coffee cup, and at the same time, Charlotte's roving hand picked up something else. His coffee went everywhere! All over the tablecloth and into the remains of the *tortoni*. Alex's eyes were big as bowling balls. Unfortunately, so was the "something else." There was no way he could escape now. He couldn't even stand up, for God's sake!

"What happened, ol' buddy?" Doug asked, but Alex could tell he didn't really want to know. Doug's eyes were still on Renee, and it didn't take much imagination to figure out what was going on under their end of the tablecloth. Shekhey was enjoying himself, too, though not quite in the same manner. He was more dignified, and so was Margo. Both of her hands were on the table. Why couldn't Margo have sat next to Alex?

So Alex sat there, rubbing feverishly at the coffee with his napkin, while Charlotte did her rubbing under cover. ... To his dismay, it began to feel good. He gave up on the coffee, and on the conversation ... and sat there like a big lump. *A big, stupid lump*, he said to himself. He hadn't really done anything yet. But he still felt guilty. Even this was unfair to Andrea. It was cheating. He sighed and closed his eyes. His elbows were on the table, and he put his head in his hands.

"Ummm, good, huh?" the low-pitched voice whispered in his ear.

God, he thought, then said aloud, "I've got to get out of here."

"Of course we do," she said.

"No, you don't understand. I'm sick," he said. "I don't feel good."

"You feel good to me," she replied.

He turned to her and looked straight into her well-dressed eyes. The time to get away was now. "Look, uh, Charlotte," he said. "You're a lovely woman and I've enjoyed … everything … up to now. But I really am sick. I've got to get out of here, and I need your help."

She took her hand away. "*My* help?"

He nodded, then whispered, "I can't exactly stand up and walk away."

Charlotte grinned. "I understand."

Alex placed a very large bill in her hand. She was quick and very smart.

"Oh, my goodness!" she cried, jumping to her feet, spilling a full glass of wine all over Alex. "This dear man is soaked and it's all my fault!"

"Yeah, no kidding," Doug said. He had a silly look on his face. Alex glared at him.

Charlotte began dabbing at Alex with a napkin and at the same time picked up her coat. When he stood, she was right up tight to him, one arm around his waist and the coat-draped arm in front. Alex desperately hoped he wouldn't be seen by anyone he knew, because he and Charlotte sure as hell didn't look like casual friends. He passed Doug a large bill to cover his meal.

"Have fun, you two," Doug said, grinning.

Alex glared at him again. But he managed to shake hands across the table with Shekhey, who was already on his feet. He told him how much he'd enjoyed the evening and the Egyptian stories, really meaning it. Then he made his escape. Finally!

"Think you'll be all right now?" Charlotte asked, once they were outside.

Alex nodded. He'd cooled down considerably. "Thanks," he said, reaching for his wallet.

She touched his hand. "It's okay," she said. "You've paid me enough. It's not often I have an evening like this, you know."

"What will you do now?"

She laughed. "I'll go home and take a cold shower, and you'd better do the same. I know you're not really sick."

"But—"

She put her fingers on his lips. "Shhh. You're a nice guy. A nice, *married* guy. Stay that way." She kissed him lightly on the cheek, then said, "Your friend must have got it all wrong. He said you'd really like this kind of evening, that he was doing you a big favor."

Alex smiled. "That was before I met Andrea," he said. He hailed her a cab and she climbed into the back seat.

"Andrea must be some woman," she said, looking up at him.

"She is." And he shut the door.

The evening had cost him a lot of money, a generous portion of his dignity, and a new suit. It had not been worth it.

~~~

Andrea settled into the big recliner in their cozy den. At her side was a mug of steaming hot coffee. She was so glad Alex had called. The sound of his voice still had the power to move her, to make her tremble, even when he was far away, even when she was irritated with him. *Funny*, she thought, *after I met Alex I never wanted anyone else. Never considered anyone else, no matter what problems we had ... not even now.*

To her, the irritation she had felt the past few weeks had been the worst problem of their married life, except how could it be a problem when Alex didn't even know about it? She'd almost decided that she was more upset with herself than with Alex, and that the week-long separation had been a blessing.

She picked up the first diary, of which she'd read about half. She'd never given much thought to diaries or journals before, but now she found them fascinating, like peeking into the most private parts of a person's life—their successes, failures, joys and frustrations. She was a bit ashamed of being a "peeker" but quickly forgave herself and opened the book.

Chapter 5

Dear Diary,
Mrs. St. John came into the sweetshop today while Tyler
and I were having tea. I was quite surprised, because my
mother's friends never *come to this area of the city. Aunt Violet*
engaged her in conversation, but I don't think she was fooled
for a minute. The lady will take great pleasure in telling my
mother....

~~~

Mrs. St. John paid an afternoon call on Millicent Alcott the very next day; and, because of it, Millicent had a "spell." Three more days passed, however, before Jenny's world exploded.

She knew it was coming, because her mother was increasingly silent and nervous, and her father kept asking what was wrong with the woman; he certainly hoped she wasn't headed for continuous vapors. Sooner or later Millicent would tell her husband.

"Aunt Violet, what are we going to do?" Jenny and Violet were in the older woman's sitting room, talking more frankly than Jenny had ever talked in her life. "I can't bear it if they blame you for this. It's all my fault."

"Jenny, dear, love is no one's fault. It simply happens. Well, maybe not so simply, in this case. Nevertheless, it has happened, and you and I will both put a brave face on it. I am a little surprised your mother has not confronted me, but then, we were never very close. I have always been the family black sheep."

"That's not true! We all love you, we do!"

"We are all family, Jenny, and English families take care of their own. My brother—your father—has very generously taken care of me all these years, but he never approved of the stand I took against our parents. Though he has never said it, I believe he finds spinsterhood a just punishment for my sin of disobedience."

"That's terrible!"

"No, it's normal behavior, Jenny. It is what is expected. Maybe someday, a hundred or more years from now, things will be different; but at this time, and in this place, propriety is all-important. Believe me, dear, your mother *will* tell your father, and together they will devise a plan to put a good face on things." She squeezed Jenny's hand. "You probably won't like the plan."

"But surely, when they see how much in love—"

Violet shook her head. "Love has nothing to do with this."

"Love has *everything* to do with this!" Jenny stood and stomped across the room.

"Be prepared, dear. Your father will never approve of Tyler Fleming."

"Why on earth not?" Jenny's eyes were darting fire.

"Because Mr. Fleming works with his hands."

"What! I'm going down there right now and—"

"No, you are not." Violet rose. "I reacted that way against my father, and see what it got me. You, dear, are going to be a perfect daughter in every way. Wait to see what your father's plan is, then we'll talk about how to achieve your goals *within the framework of that plan*. It will take patience, and that is something you must never forget; but, in the end, everyone's dignity will be preserved." She put her arm around her niece's shoulder. "I don't want to see you ostracized or separated from your parents in any way. You need them, Jenny, and they need you. They are good people. Very good people."

Jenny's defiant chin relaxed somewhat. "All right," she said after a moment. "I'll do as you say. Patience, however, is not one of my virtues."

Violet's smile was an anxious one.

~~~

Barclay Alcott chose to discuss Jenny's "situation" in the dining room over roast lamb and pudding, after the servants had been dismissed. In his hand was a glass of excellent wine, of which only he was permitted to partake. His face was flushed, but he tried to maintain a sense of decorum, as he addressed his daughter.

"Your mother tells me you have been meeting that young carpenter." .

"Mr. Fleming is an architect."

"He builds things. The point is, you have been seeing him against my wishes."

"You didn't expressly forbid me, Father," Jenny politely replied. "You only said I should learn to love Angus Newton."

Mr. Alcott set his wine glass down with a little more force than he intended. A few drops slid over the edge, staining the damask cloth. "Is that not the same thing?"

Jenny glanced at Aunt Violet, then bit her tongue.

"Well, is that not the same thing?" he demanded again. "If you are learning to love Angus Newton, you cannot be seen traipsing about London with a carpenter."

"Barclay," Violet injected, "if I may speak in Jenny's defense…"

"You may damn well keep your mouth shut, Violet. It seems to me you have been encouraging this transgression, if not causing it!"

Millicent gasped and held her handkerchief to her forehead.

"Forgive me, my dear," Mr. Alcott said to his wife, with some difficulty. "I did promise to remain calm." He took another sip of his wine and cleared his throat before speaking. His tone was patronizing. "Now then, Violet, what do you wish to say?"

"Only that Jenny's chance meetings with Mr. Fleming were always properly chaperoned."

"*Chance* meetings?"

"Yes, Father," Jenny responded. "They were never prearranged."

"I find that hard to believe."

"Nevertheless, it is true."

"In that case, it seems the young man knows your schedule a little too well." He pressed his fingertips together; and, as he formulated his plan, his voice gradually rose in pitch and volume. He just couldn't help himself. "Therefore," he said, "you will change the time of your dancing lesson, beginning with the next one ... and you will not enter that bloody sweet shop again!"

Jenny's mother fairly swooned.

"Oh, Millicent, enough vapors! Jenny, have I made myself clear?"

Jenny glanced at her aunt, who nodded imperceptibly. "Yes, Father," she replied.

Mr. Alcott leaned forward and stared at his daughter without blinking. "If this does not correct our little situation, I will take more drastic measures. Be certain of that."

~~~

The following week Jenny took her dance lesson at a new time. Tyler Fleming, of course, was nowhere to be seen. The next week, however, he was strolling toward the studio as she and Violet emerged. His clothing was immaculate, and he carried a walking stick—for effect, of course. Jenny was enthralled.

"Well now," he said, tipping his hat. "Imagine meeting you two lovely ladies on such a fine morning. Why, I was saying to Madame Dupré just the other day that I probably needed to get out a bit earlier to enjoy this good weather. She was kind enough to suggest that this would be a perfect time," he added with a wink.

"Oh, Tyler!" Jenny laughed. She was beyond blushing at his delightfully naughty contrivances. "We were just going beyond the sweet shop to the outdoor café in the next block. I suppose we couldn't stop you, if you wished to visit the same establishment."

"I suppose not. Shall I walk behind you?" He was teasing.

But Violet said, "That would be a very good idea, Mr. Fleming. In fact, ten minutes behind us would be ideal." She took Jenny by the elbow and started along.

"Oh, wait!" Tyler called suddenly. "Wait just a moment!"

The ladies turned to see him dash across to the other side of the street. The crossing-sweepers had just been through to clear the path, so he tipped them the customary coppers before turning his attention to the waif-like flower girl who was selling violets. Jenny had never paid much attention to flower girls, but she thought this one was a pretty little thing, despite her bedraggled skirts and shawl, the worn-out shoes, and the unbecoming black straw hat. Her smile was bright.

"'Ere ya are!" the girl cried, so loudly that the ladies could hear her across the street. "A fine bunch!"

Tyler paid her and hurried back. "For you, m'lady," he said, presenting them to Violet with an elaborate bow. "Violets for Aunt Violet."

Jenny giggled.

Violet gave an exasperated sigh, though any fool could tell she was pleased. She accepted the tiny bouquet with thanks and ushered Jenny along toward the café. Jenny looked over her shoulder at Tyler. It was her turn to wink.

Seated at a table in the back, well off the street and shaded by a tree, they ordered tea and scones with clotted cream and waited for Mr. Fleming's "unexpected" arrival.

"I knew he would find me, Aunt Violet! I knew it!"

Violet sighed and looked around the nearly empty courtyard. "This makes me decidedly uneasy, Jenny. If Mrs. St. John found us at the sweet shop, she or someone else will surely find us here. You realize her appearance was not accidental. She had heard rumors, and rumors will start again."

"Oh, bother the rumors!"

"You won't say that if your father has to come up with another plan. He means to keep you two apart, Jenny."

"But I *love* Tyler!"

"That is exactly the problem."

Just then Tyler stepped through the gate and looked around. He was properly startled, of course, to see two acquaintances—Miss Violet Alcott and the lovely Miss Jenny Alcott. With a genteel greeting, he moved forward and was invited to join the ladies for tea.

Seated, he quickly leaned toward Jenny and spoke softly. "I knew something was amiss when Madame Dupré said your lesson time had been changed."

"Oh, Tyler, what are we to do?"

Violet busied herself with her scones.

"Well, you can be sure this won't work a second time," he said, keeping his voice low. "And it is just as well. Seeing you like this is torture. I need to touch you, Jenny. I want to take you in my arms and kiss you, right this minute!"

Jenny clapped her hand over her mouth to stifle a giggle and glanced at her aunt.

"Don't mind me," Violet said. "I am suddenly hard of hearing." She rose and walked slowly toward the gate.

"Jenny, I have got to see you in private," Tyler whispered. "I cannot bear this grief any longer. Can you get away this evening, so that we can talk? Perhaps in one of your gardens after dark?"

Jenny's heart began beating very fast. *Sneak out of the house?* She had never done such a thing before, not even with her best friend, Evelyn. But she remembered Tyler's kisses and answered quickly.

"In the rose garden," she whispered, "at midnight." Her eyes sparkled with excitement. She had chosen midnight because it sounded romantic.

The Rose Garden

Chapter 6

"Ah, Jenny," Andrea said aloud. "I'm afraid I know where you're heading." She sighed, pushed herself out of the recliner, and went to the kitchen to warm her coffee. It was a matter of being a child one day and an adult the next. There wasn't any "in between." Jenny would learn fast, and where would it lead her?

Andrea could guess at one possibility. Rules and restrictions had forced her to sneak around, too. She'd been eighteen, just graduated from high school. By today's standards, eighteen was old and eighteen-year-olds didn't sneak. They just did it. But things were different then. The sexual revolution was still a ways off. The most daring thing Andrea Cooper and her friends had ever done was smoke pastel-colored cigarettes behind the big Jameson marker at the cemetery. The sneaking was kind of exciting, but the smoking made them all sick.

But then she tried something else. His name was Roger Overby, and he was an artist. Her mother called him a "beatnik," a term Andrea hadn't understood but guessed it meant someone irresponsible. But he wasn't. He was just different. His hair was a little long and his clothes weren't what boys wore to church, which is the only place Andrea's mother ever saw boys. Roger was special. He had gone to art school, and that was exactly what Andrea wanted to do. She wanted to be a "great artist," and she was certain that if she just had some training to go with her talent and determination, she could be exactly that—a great artist. She had wanted it more than anything.

"But you can't earn a living painting pictures," her father had said, "unless you mean to teach school. Is that what you mean, Andrea? To be a school teacher?"

"Well ... no, not really. Public schools aren't offering art classes much anymore," she answered. "They're leaning toward math and science, so there probably won't be a need for art teachers a few years from now."

"Then what on earth good would art school do you, Andrea?" her mother chimed in. "That's frivolous. A waste of good, hard-earned money, and you know how hard your father has worked all his life for his money. Seems to me that math and science would be a smarter choice. You are a smart girl, aren't you?"

"Money isn't everything, Mother," Andrea dared to say.

"True, but a body can't do without it either, and we certainly can't support you all your life. It's best you rid yourself of romantic notions."

"Now, Doris," her father had said, "no need to be so harsh." Henry Cooper was forever softening his wife's brittle tongue, even more so since he'd been bedridden with terminal cancer. Still, he was a force to be reckoned with, especially to Doris, because they both believed in a literal interpretation of the Bible (the King James Version, that is, which in their minds was the only *real* Bible), where it says that the man is the head of the household and all others must be subservient to him. Doris always caved in. It was her duty. But she had ways of swaying Henry to her point of view.

"It's for Andrea's own good," she said to her husband. "She's got to be able to take care of herself once you're gone, because God knows I haven't the means nor the ability. I've done nothing else in my life except be a good wife to you and a good mother to her. I'm not trained for anything. Truth be known, Andrea may have to take care of me one day."

"Now Doris," Henry said, "there's plenty of insurance to take care of you." He sighed a long sigh. "But your mother is right, Andrea.

You need to make a stable life for yourself, just in case you don't find a husband." Andrea winced. "Choose a good, solid occupation and save your money. Art can be a hobby. It's what it should be."

Andrea's parents had made it clear that they preferred Calvary Bible College in Huntsville for her education. But its rules and restrictions reminded her of articles she'd read about Bob Jones University in South Carolina. Regarding the *dating parlor*: "The spacious top-floor lobby with uncomfortable couches and chairs looks like a furniture showroom. Sour-faced chaperones sitting atop survey towers keep an eye on the students at all times." She did not want any part of that kind of environment!

Andrea's hopes were sinking fast; and, as the weeks passed, so was her father. She dreaded being left alone with her mother. But maybe that wouldn't be so bad. They did have good times mixing up wonderful things in the big farm kitchen. She had to hold onto that.

One night in his weakened, but still lucid, condition, Andrea's father called her to his bedside.

"Promise me, Andrea, that you'll go to a real college and make something of yourself," he whispered. "You're plenty smart enough to get in. The money's there. I've been saving since you were born. It's for you, my darling child. Promise?"

She held his hand and wept because she loved him. He had been a good father, and she would miss him terribly. So she promised. She promised because she wanted to please him in his dying moments, but she never honestly believed she'd be held to that promise. She could support herself as an artist. She knew she could. All she needed was the chance to study, to learn how to do it.

After her father died, she approached her mother once more. Doris, however, now in control as head of the household, was more prim, proper, and unyielding than ever before.

"There's no question of going to art school," she said. "You made a promise in the eyes of God, Andrea Jane, and you must keep it. You'll end up in hell if you don't. I'll not pay for art school. Only a real college degree, as your father wished."

"It's my money, you know."

"But I say how it will be spent."

"May I spend it on an economics education at Georgia State?" Andrea had thought very carefully about her alternatives.

Her mother looked at her, warily. "What's that?"

"I'll go into the financial field. You won't have to worry about money ever again."

So Andrea Cooper applied for admission to the economics department at Georgia State in Atlanta. She was accepted. She would graduate from high school in the spring, then enter in the fall.

But that was the summer Roger Overby came to town. He was staying with his uncle, helping on the farm, trying to earn enough money to go to Paris. An art school graduate! He said Paris was the only place in the world to become a real artist. Andrea thought he was wonderful. Imagine—going to Paris, living in a garret (like in the movies), and painting for a living! The whole idea was romantic. And so was Roger.

… And because of Roger Overby and that wild and wonderful summer, another full year passed before Andrea could begin her studies at Georgia State.

~~~

Barclay Alcott was still working in his study when Jenny gathered up her skirts and stole down the back stairway. She wasn't worried about him, since her father had no reason to suspect she was awake. She always retired early. Besides, she was carrying her shoes to be sure she made no noise. The servants had gone to their quarters two hours before. She chose the side exit at the end of the lower hall. It was away from everything and seldom used. Only one dim gaslight burned outside the door. She moved quickly.

When she was safely outside, with the door shut behind her, she slipped into her walking shoes and hurried toward the shadows of the huge birch trees. The rose garden was at the far end, just past the statuary. Jenny had never been in the gardens at night, let alone at *midnight*, and she found the statues intimidating, even eerie, with moonlight behind them. She stopped momentarily, taking a deep breath. Had she done the right thing, agreeing to meet Tyler like this? She was a little nervous, but too excited to turn back. Bravely, she lifted her chin and strode through the statuary to the small garden gate.

"Jenny!" Tyler was waiting. He came to her with his arms outstretched, and she no longer had doubts. She ran the remaining few steps.

"Oh, my darling," he said, holding her tightly to himself. "I've waited for this for too many long weeks, ever since the night of your party." He kissed her mouth tenderly and longingly, again and again. "Daytime tea with your Aunt Violet was fine," he said between kisses, "but hardly enough. Oh, Jenny, I love you!" he cried aloud.

"Be quiet, Tyler," Jenny whispered. "Someone may hear us!"

"It's midnight, my love. Even the devil has gone to bed!"

He kissed her again, before she could say a word—and she wanted to tell him she loved him! Well, she'd just have to show him. She returned his kisses fervently, using all her strength to push her lips into his. Even so, she was surprised when she felt his tongue probing her mouth. What was he doing? But, oh, it was delicious! She parted her lips slightly, then more, awakening to the most incredible feelings—feelings that far surpassed anything Evelyn had described! "Squishy," indeed!

They sat on the wooden bench a long time, talking and kissing. Finally, Tyler said, I have a surprise for you, Jenny."

Her eyes widened. "What is it?"

"Theatre tickets," he said, pulling them from his coat pocket. "Tickets to Oscar Wilde's comedy at the St. James Theatre next Saturday night. It's titled *Lady Windermere's Fan*." He grinned. "Should be interesting."

Jenny sighed. "Tyler, you know I can't go to the theatre with you, no matter how much I want to."

"Not with me, darling, with your Aunt Violet." He handed two tickets to her and held up a third. "I just happen to have the seat next to yours," he added, eyes twinkling.

Jenny buried her laughter in his chest.

"I am going to hold your hand the entire evening," he said. "You see, even a comedy can be romantic." After one more kiss he stood, pulling her to her feet. "Now I want you to go back to the house before someone notices you are gone."

"You said even the devil is asleep at midnight."

"I shall feel much better with you safely tucked into bed. Just wish it could be my bed," he added, hugging her. Suddenly, his hand came around and cupped her breast.

"Oh, Tyler!" Jenny was completely surprised.

His hand lingered a moment, then he released her, saying, "Go, dearest, before I lose my senses." He opened the little gate. "And I won't see you after your lesson on Thursday. From what you have told me of your father's 'spies,' I think it best."

"'Til ... 'til Saturday then," she said, still dazed by the unexpected touch.

Gently, he pushed her through the gate.

He touched my breast! she thought as she hurried through the statuary. *He touched my breast*! And, later, as she lay awake on her down-stuffed pillow ... it still tingled.

~~~

The aisle seat on Jenny's left remained empty, as she and Aunt Violet waited for the play to begin.

"You should have told me before this!" Violet spoke firmly but softly, so as not to draw attention. "I thought there were just two tickets, one for you and one for me. And now you say Tyler Fleming will be sitting *there*." She pointed a gloved finger. "Really, Jenny, this was unfair of you."

Violet had been excited about seeing Mr. Wilde's play and grateful for the opportunity, since tickets were difficult to obtain. She had worn her very best theatre costume—an elegant creation in deep purple, her favorite color. That and the sparkle in her emerald eyes made her look half her age. But now, some of the excitement was gone, because Violet was angry with Jenny.

"It was wrong of me, I know," Jenny said quickly. "But I was so afraid if I told you about Tyler you would have said no, that we should not come."

"I probably would have said no. This is so ... so public. It is exactly the kind of prank that will land you in big trouble!" Violet's normally gentle voice was reduced to a hiss. "I'm beginning to think Mr. Fleming is not all he seems; otherwise, he would have more consideration for you and your reputation."

Jenny felt guilty. She knew she had a selfish streak, but she did not want to think of Tyler in that way. All of his little indiscretions were because he loved her! Still, Aunt Violet was the only stronghold in her life right now, the only person to whom she could cling, who kept her sane.

"I'm sorry for deceiving you, truly I am," she said. And she meant it. But she wasn't at all sorry that Tyler would be sitting next to her. Where was he? She wanted to turn around, to look for him, but she didn't dare. Their meeting had to appear accidental.

There was still no sign of Tyler when the lights went down, and Jenny began to worry. Had he forgotten? Could that be possible? In just a few moments, however, she felt a rustling at her side, and he was there, whispering in her ear, "I love you, Jenny!" And all was well. Oh, very well indeed, as he took her hand and slowly peeled off her glove. It was deliciously disconcerting, making her feel almost naked. As his strong hand wrapped itself around her bare fingers, a prickly sensation shot through her body. And to think they would be there together for the entire evening!

She guessed the play was good. She honestly didn't pay much attention to anything except Tyler's hand playing with her fingers, and his shoulder rubbing against hers, and the occasional brush of his lips against her ear. It was hard to concentrate, but she managed to keep her eyes forward and to laugh when the rest of the audience laughed. Violet, thank goodness, was fully absorbed in the play.

Just before the end of the first act, Tyler left. "I shall return after the second act starts," he said, "after the lights go out. It's better that no one notices us."

Reluctantly, she let him release her hand, though she was inwardly thankful for his consideration.

When the lights went on at intermission, she and Violet rose and stepped into the aisle … coming face-to-face with Barclay Alcott! He had a wide smile pasted on his lips, but his eyes were steaming with rage as he said, "Good evening, my dear. Good evening, Violet. Shall we take the air together?"

Jenny had no choice. She and Violet followed her father into the "air" and straight into his waiting carriage!

Not one word was spoken all the way home. By the time they were ushered into Barclay's study, Jenny was drenched in tears and Violet had twisted her lace handkerchief into a rag.

Chapter 7

"Please don't blame Aunt Violet," Jenny begged. "She did not know that Tyler would be there. Honestly! She scolded me something awful when she found out."

"Violet? Is this true?"

Violet sighed and nodded her head.

"Go to your room then. You are out of this."

"But Barclay—"

"Go, Violet, while my temper is still intact."

Violet went.

"Now, Miss, can you offer any excuse at all for your wretched behavior?"

"No, Father." But then Jenny became very brave. "How did you happen to be there?" she asked.

"I bought a ticket when I knew you would be going."

"Then you were not there to see the play."

"I was there to see what devilment you might be up to."

Jenny lifted her chin high. "You were spying on me?"

"Dammit, girl! You are barely sixteen years old, and you have given me little reason to trust you lately!"

"We were not doing anything wrong."

"Being seen in public with that carpenter was wrong!"

"Would it be all right if I were to see him in private?"

"Sit down, you exasperating child! And stop talking back to me. You may not see that young man again under *any* circumstance."

Jenny sat. Her father sat beside her and said, more gently, "Your mother and I want only what is best for you, my dear, and that is Angus Newton as your husband. He is certainly willing, and he will provide you with a title as well as wealth. Your entire life will be free of worry."

"Angus Newton is a goose."

Barclay Alcott sighed. "Mr. Fleming has no prospects."

"But I love him! Father, I think about him all the time we're apart, and my heart aches for want of him. Please, Father, please—I want to marry Tyler Fleming!"

Mr. Alcott leaned back against the divan. "I see. And has Mr. Fleming asked you to marry him?"

"Well ... in so many words."

The room was silent for what seemed an eternity to the young girl on the threshold of womanhood. Her father's face was frighteningly calm. Calm before the storm? She sat very still, except for her shaking knees. Thank God for voluminous skirts! What was going through his mind? Would he be impressed by Tyler's good intentions?

Finally, her father pushed himself to his feet and said, "Jenny, for your own good I must stand by my decision. Therefore, you leave me no choice. For the next two weeks you will be confined to this house ... and you may consider your dancing lessons canceled, permanently." He turned and went out the door, leaving Jenny in a state of devastation.

~~~

During her two weeks of detention, Jenny did the only thing she could do, the only thing she felt like doing—she threw herself into her ballet exercises, stretching and turning her body to its limits and then some; and in her mind, with each short, sharp *frappé*, she kicked herself and her situation. Why did things have to be this way? *Frappé.*

Why were her parents so old-fashioned? *Frappé.* Marriages were being arranged less and less these days. Happiness ought to count for something, for heaven's sake! *Frappé, frappé!*

To ease her heartache, she tried to block Tyler Fleming from her mind and concentrate on dance. Lessons or no lessons, she would not give up her dream of becoming a ballerina, no matter what her father said or did. She would *never* give that up. She had not really thought about how Tyler would fit into her plans. He just would. Somehow.

Each day she worked very hard, reviewing over and over the things Madame Dupré had taught her. She still had not decided if she wanted to be a "serious" dancer, like the legendary Marie Taglioni, or outrageously exciting, like Loie Fuller. Madame Dupré, of course, was interested in classical dance. She did not have much time for the likes of Loie Fuller. "Too many props, not enough technique," she had said. "Anyone can do that." Jenny wasn't at all sure that anyone could. It looked extremely difficult, especially all that business with the flowing skirts and how they caught just the right lights at just the right time. Loie Fuller was spectacular; and, oh, how the audiences loved her! Jenny Alcott wanted to be loved, too.

One morning near the end of the first week, there was a light tap on the door of "Jenny's Studio," as everyone referred to her practice room, and Evelyn slipped in, quickly shutting the door.

Jenny's eyes opened wide. "Evelyn! How did you—"

"Shh! It was easy. I brought a length of green muslin for the kitchen maid." Evelyn spoke quietly. "I just *had* to find out what happened. What on earth did you do that was terrible enough to get yourself confined?"

"You are the terrible one," Jenny replied, smiling. "Bribing a kitchen maid!" Delighted, she pulled Evelyn to the corner where they sat on the floor, backs to the wall.

"Well ... tell! Honestly, Jenny, I can't imagine what you could have—" She stopped short. "Uh-oh! Did they find out about you and Tyler meeting at the sweet shop?"

"Worse. We met at the theatre and Father was there."

"Oooooh, no!" Evelyn squealed, properly impressed. So Jenny told her about the fateful night, about her father's reaction, and about her canceled dance lessons.

"Oh, posh! Don't worry about the lessons. He will relent soon enough. But about Tyler, now—oh my, how romantic! Jenny, whatever will you do?"

Jenny sighed. "I have no idea. Aunt Violet says to wait and see what happens after my two weeks are up. She's angry with me, too. I guess I'll wait. I just hope Tyler understands that this is not my choice."

"Of course he will! Oh, Jenny, has he talked about love?"

Jenny blushed. "He does love me. He said so."

Evelyn squealed again. "Will you marry him? Has he asked you?"

" ... Sort of. I think he will. If I ever get to see him again," she added, propping her chin on her knees.

"This is *marvelous*—even better than a novel!"

"You would not say that if you were the one confined."

"Oh, yes I would!" Evelyn replied. "Tyler is a marvelous looking man, and I'll bet he can really kiss!" Jenny blushed again, and Evelyn lowered her voice. "Has he touched your breasts yet?"

"Evelyn! That is none of your business."

"He has! He has! I knew it! Isn't it marvelous? Oh, Jenny, if you marry him, you must tell me all about what married people do when they are alone in the bedroom. I can't ask just *anyone*, and I am dying to know."

Jenny was suddenly horrified. She hadn't even thought about *that*, only about how nice it would be to live in the same house and go out together. And to kiss, of course.

"I'm not exactly sure what it is they do," Evelyn went on, "but I know that ladies are not supposed to like it." She leaned closer and whispered gleefully, "If it's anything at all like having your breasts touched, you can be sure *I* will like it!"

Later that night alone in bed, Jenny thought for a long time about Evelyn's comments. Would she like it? Whatever *it* was. Suddenly, a warm glow ignited in her body, just from thinking about it. She felt the glow creep slowly in all directions from somewhere deep inside, and by the time it had engulfed her, she knew she would. She would like it very much!

~~~

The following Thursday afternoon, Violet came into Jenny's studio and sat in the straight-backed chair by the window. It was the only piece of furniture in the bare room, except for the ballet bar on one wall and mirrors on the other. She often sat there watching Jenny practice, sometimes even coaching, reminding Jenny of things Madame Dupré had said during lessons. Often, too, as on this day, she would bring her crochet basket.

"What are you making now?" Jenny asked, between turns.

"A handkerchief for your wedding."

Jenny stopped in her tracks. "What did you say?"

"You heard me. A handkerchief for your wedding. You do plan to marry someday, don't you?"

"Yes, of course, but—"

"Then you will need a beautiful, lace-trimmed handkerchief to carry. All brides do."

Jenny's eyes filled with tears as she crossed the room and sat on the floor at Violet's feet. "Oh, Aunt Violet," she said, "I want to marry Tyler. I really do."

"I know, dear. Despite my misgivings about the young man, do you recall my advice? That you must have patience? It is still good advice."

"I am not so sure. Sometimes I want to run away and never come back." Her gaze shifted beyond Violet, out the window and across the gardens, through the perennial fog, toward the rose garden. She would never forget the rose garden.

"Running away is not the answer," her aunt said.

"Then what is?"

Violet stopped her busy hands. "You must stay in your father's good graces. He will relent on the ballet lessons, believe me. He knows that dancing gives you great pleasure; and, whether you care to believe it or not, he truly does love you beneath all of his stuffiness and bluster. He told me once, 'It's excellent exercise. Jenny will always be healthy.'" Violet had imitated Barclay's gruff voice, and Jenny could not help smiling just a little.

"Also," Violet continued, "Millicent secretly enjoys the attention your dancing gets. She's no fool. She can see that her friends are envious, because it is a tiny bit daring, and because their daughters do not have what it takes. Though they brush it off as frivolity, they are always asking questions, which Millicent takes great delight in answering."

"*My* mother?"

"Your mother."

Jenny considered that. "I have always wondered why my dancing didn't seem to produce 'spells,'" she said finally.

Violet suppressed a smile. "Now, about Tyler Fleming," she said, resting her work in her lap. "He is an intelligent and resourceful young man. I suggest you let him deal with your problem."

"Tyler?"

"Yes, Tyler. If he *truly* loves you, as you seem to think he does, he certainly is not going to give up at the first sign of resistance. Well, actually, this is the third, isn't it?" she added wryly, and Jenny smiled. "My Samuel didn't give up at first," Violet went on. "I was the one who wilted like a flower on the vine. I turned inward and refused to see him again, as my father wished. Finally, Samuel stopped coming by. He thought I had fallen out of love. A dear friend of mine told me later that he was heartbroken … and that broke *my* heart." Her sigh was barely audible.

"I am so sorry," Jenny said kindly.

"It's all in the past, dear. It is the present that concerns us. Now then, you must give Tyler some room to be the man that he is … or is not. You must allow him the privilege of taking the initiative."

"But … but, will he?"

"Of course. He already has."

Jenny sat up straighter on the floor, her heart suddenly racing.

"In what way?"

"He has sent you a letter, outlining his plan." Violet reached into her crochet basket. "It's a good plan, too. Especially good because it does not involve *me*." She looked at Jenny and smiled. "He asked me to read it before giving it to you."

"You saw him? When? Where?" Jenny was on her knees now.

"I happened to stop by a certain charming little café the other morning for tea and scones, and Mr. Fleming happened to be there." Jenny threw her arms around her aunt and hugged her. "The letter," she said quickly. "Where is it?"

Violet pulled an envelope from her basket and handed it over.

Chapter 8

Andrea reached for her mug, but the coffee was stone cold. *No wonder*, she thought, glancing at the grandfather clock in the corner. *It's nearly midnight!* She had been reading for hours. Jenny's handwriting was clear but cramped, as if she'd wanted to use every smidgen of space for her complicated thoughts and feelings and her detailed accounting of events. Jenny had been very thorough, and that was taking Andrea a great deal of time. She didn't mind, though. She was fascinated. She wanted to learn all she could about the young woman who had lived in her house and danced in her attic.

At least Tyler moved slowly, Andrea thought. He wasn't scaring Jenny to death in the process of seduction, at least so far. She was convinced that seduction was exactly what it was, because something about Tyler Fleming simply did not ring true. Violet had sensed it, too. Was such slow motion typical of young people in the nineteenth century? Did they "put a face on things," as their elders did?

Roger Overby had moved slowly, too; but it was a little different, because there were no declarations of love. He and Andrea simply enjoyed each other—every bit of each other—for an entire summer. Andrea had never felt "used," as her mother called it later. It had been a mutual giving and taking between friends. The only game they had to play was the game of hiding their involvement, because, after all, "What would people think?" Roger knew that Mrs. Cooper (no outsider *ever* called Andrea's mother Doris) did not approve of him, so he made it a point to stay out of her way.

"It's not that she doesn't like you, Roger," Andrea had said. "It's just your ... the way you ..."

"I know," he offered with a smile. "Mrs. Cooper has a set of nice, neat little boxes that she puts people in. I don't fit into any of her boxes." That was a good description of Doris Cooper's attitude. That and the fact that everything she did was according to the will of God. Who can argue with the will of God?

"It's okay, Andrea," he said. "I don't worry about it. She has a right to her opinions."

Roger understood a lot of things. He understood Andrea's need to break out of the cocoon, and he was gentle and kind in every way. She did not love him, but she admired him.

They remained friends after the summer ended. After Roger went to Paris they were pen pals for a time, but as the years passed, their correspondence dwindled to Christmas cards only. Then one spring, after Andrea had truly grown up and had begun her career, Roger returned to the States for a visit. They had dinner together and realized in a very short time that they no longer had much in common. Roger was living a carefree life—very little money and not much future— and he was happy. Andrea was tied to the clock and calendar, had money in the bank and a promotion on the horizon. She supposed she was happy. She didn't think too much about it.

So they said good-bye and the Christmas cards stopped. And Roger Overby never knew what a profound effect their teenage summer had had on Andrea Cooper. It had established what she was. It had also determined what she could never be.

She stretched in her chair, thinking about refilling the mug. She was tired of sitting, but she certainly wasn't sleepy, and she had nearly finished the first book. Standing, she turned the page for a quick peek at what she would read next. As she did, a letter came away from the fragile pages. It was yellowed with age and some of the flowing script was smeared; nevertheless, it was readable. It was Tyler's letter, the one Violet had handed to Jenny that day in the studio. Andrea forgot all about her coffee.

> *My dearest Jenny,*
> *I have been tortured with thoughts of you, ever since the night you vanished from the theatre. I asked myself, what was your fate? I knew immediately that something was terribly amiss, but only when Madame Dupré informed me of your canceled lessons did I know for sure that your father must have discovered us and whisked you away! Oh, my darling! If I could only undo the damage and relieve your suffering! Still, I cannot conceive of journeying through this life without you. I love you, dearest Jenny, and I will not give up easily.*
> *I shall take matters into my own hands, visiting your father on the morrow. I shall talk with him, man to man, concerning a proper courting. Pray for me as I undertake this paradoxical task—unpleasant in facing your father, but most pleasant in its reason. Whatever the outcome, I shall pass word through your Aunt Violet, and we will proceed from there at that time. I cherish memories of roses and you.*
> *Yours forever,*
> *Tyler*

~~~

In her bedroom, Jenny read the letter over and over, sometimes smiling in joy, sometimes weeping in despair. Occasionally, a tear would find its way to the page, and she would blot it away, careful not to smear the ink too much. It was her very first love letter, and it meant everything to her. She was sure she would not sleep a wink, worrying about the coming confrontation between Tyler and her father.

Should she sneak downstairs and try to listen? Should she hide away in her room? Should she go for a walk in the park? When the time finally came, she decided to work in her studio, dancing until she dropped from exhaustion. She was asleep there on the floor when

Violet came in.

"Wake up, dear," Violet said, gently shaking her. "It's time to dress for dinner."

"Tyler? Is he … ?"

"He's gone. He left hours ago."

"And … "

"I don't know. I could not very well eavesdrop. However, your parents were closeted in the study for a long time, then they went out for a drive in the carriage and stayed the entire afternoon, only returning a few moments ago."

"Is that a good sign?"

"I couldn't say. But I suspect dinner will be somewhat of an ordeal. You must look your best, dear, and be strong."

Upstairs, Violet helped button her into a lovely blue muslin, which Jenny had embroidered herself, and brushed her long dark hair until it shone. She looked like a young woman of confidence, but she was extremely nervous. The situation was intimidating. And, as she finally descended the stairs to take her seat at the enormous mahogany dinner table, she was even further intimidated by the sour-faced portraits of men in ruffs lining the side wall. They strongly resembled her father.

Her father, however, was not sour-faced this evening. He was extremely pleasant. Throughout the meal he was considerate, even solicitous, of Jenny, Violet and Millicent. He was so nice that Jenny wanted to scream in frustration. Why didn't he get on with it? Had Tyler been successful? Is that why her father was being so nice? Or were the pleasantries meant to cushion the blow that would surely follow?

"Ladies, we have something to discuss," he said, finally, over dessert.

Here it comes, Jenny thought. *He will discuss Tyler's visit.* She was more than nervous now; she was scared nearly to death! To keep her hands from shaking, she clasped them tightly beneath the table.

"As you know, Millicent has been in ill health for quite some time." He was addressing Jenny and Violet. Millicent stared demurely at her plate. "Her spells have been more frequent of late," he continued, "and, after a long consultation with Doctor Stuart this afternoon, we have decided to take the steps necessary for regaining her health."

What in the world is he talking about? Jenny knew, and so did everyone else, that her mother's "vapors" were convenient escape mechanisms. There was not a thing wrong with her!

"Doctor Stuart has prescribed a long rest in a place known for its healing air. Many people have testified that it is a remarkable place for taking a cure, due to the mild climate and pine aroma. So, ladies, we have made arrangements for the four of us to spend the next six months in the Colonies. Georgia, to be precise. A lovely little town, Doctor Stuart says, near the Florida border. He has been there himself. Plantation country. Good quail hunting, I'm told."

Jenny was speechless.

"S-six months?" Violet asked.

Barclay nodded. "It will take at least that long for Millicent's cure. Won't it, dear?" he added, patting his wife's hand.

"We're going ... across the ocean?" Jenny asked, finding and biting her tongue at the same time. "To live?" She was horrified.

"That is right, my dear. Our solicitor is making the arrangements. He assures me that a lovely, furnished house will be available to us." Then he added with an extra-sweet smile, "I'm told there is an excellent ballet teacher in the area—Catherine Kingsley. A former student of, uh ... of Katti Lanner, I believe?"

A carrot. He was handing Jenny a carrot! Oh, it was a pretty carrot to be sure—she would be fortunate indeed to work with a student of Katti Lanner, the Empire's renowned ballet mistress and choreographer. And she had heard of Catherine Kingsley—not a famous dancer, but a good one who had worked regularly in London. Given Jenny's situation, it was probably the opportunity of her lifetime, not only in what she could learn, but in the connections she would be able to make. Why, by the time they returned to London, she might even be granted an audience with Katti Lanner herself!

But what of Tyler? Jenny's elation suddenly plummeted. Why

didn't her father mention his visit? Jenny could not mention it because she was not supposed to know about it. She glanced at Aunt Violet, whose eyes told her to keep quiet. She looked at her mother, but Millicent still had an unnatural interest in her plate.

The journey was contrived, of course, to get Jenny away from Tyler Fleming. But perhaps it wasn't a bad idea, she thought, if Tyler would wait for her, and she was sure he would. Her spirits rose once again. Not only would she have a marvelous opportunity to launch her career, which her father still did not take seriously, but six months might be just enough time for Angus Newton to find another bride! That Ada Gregory had been simpering after him forever. Evelyn could help Ada along—Jenny would ask her to!

She swallowed hard, forcing down her ambivalent feelings along with her pride. "That's fine, Father," she replied sweetly. "Mother's health must take priority over everything." Millicent was still focused on her plate, looking a bit embarrassed, Jenny thought. *And well she should!*

"I am so glad you agree, my dear," Barclay said. "You ladies shall spend the next few weeks preparing for the journey—get yourselves some new clothes, things suitable for a warm climate, and instruct the servants to pack whatever personal items you would like to take. And Violet," he added, pointedly, "I expect you to keep Jenny very busy during this time of preparation. There is much to be done, and no time to be wasted." Violet couldn't possibly have missed his meaning. Jenny certainly didn't.

~~~

"I was very proud of you," Violet said, as she helped Jenny out of her dress. "Six months isn't such a long time to be away."

"It is an exceedingly long time to be away from Tyler, but I can endure it, because in the end I believe it will improve every facet of our situation. When I explain it to Tyler, he will understand and wait for me. I know he will!"

"Jenny, dear, Tyler is—"

"Wait, Aunt Violet. Please just listen to my idea." She spoke quickly of her excitement about working with Catherine Kingsley, about the possibility of meeting Katti Lanner, and, best of all, about doing a little matchmaking between Angus Newton and Ada Gregory. With Evelyn's help, of course. "With Angus out of the way," she went on, "Tyler will have a better chance of winning Father over, because there is not one other old goose on the horizon that Father would deem suitable for me. Not one!"

Violet wasn't so sure about that, but she couldn't help laughing aloud at Jenny's spirit. "As your friend, Evelyn, would say, 'A *marvelous* idea.'"

"And just imagine—through Katti Lanner I could have the chance to become an Empire ballerina! It is the opportunity of a lifetime! Tyler would·be so proud! But we must let him know what has happened, and I want to know what went on between him and my father. I have got to see him!"

"Now, Jenny, you heard your father's orders to me. I am to keep you very busy. That means no little excursions into neighborhood cafés, and no wandering out of my sight."

"Then go by yourself," Jenny pleaded. "You could at least take a message from me. And bring one back."

Violet sighed—she was sighing a lot lately—then she looked into Jenny's bright eyes and relented. "One message," she said. "Just one."

~~~

During the next several days the ladies sorted through bolts of material and endured being measured and pinned, all with an eye toward comfort and fashion. They ordered several shawls in paisley and silk; there were shirtwaists to be made, and dresses with leg-of-mutton sleeves. Millicent ordered a new *capuchin*, which she promised to loan Violet for an evening out, though Violet could not imagine what kind of "evening out" she could have by herself.

Evelyn insisted Jenny purchase some white shoes with long,

pointed toes, so stylish now. "I suppose your mother will take her Adelaide boots," she said, rolling her eyes. "They must have belonged to her grandmother!"

"They probably did," Jenny answered, "but mother likes fur. She'll never give them up."

"I wonder if you'll see men wearing those Levi trousers in the Colonies?" Evelyn whispered, grinning widely.

"We are not going out *West*," Jenny said with a laugh. Lowering her voice she added, "And we should not be discussing men's trousers." That comment sent Evelyn into an absolute fit of giggles.

While dressmakers worked, Violet and Millicent busied the servants with packing. They even had Jenny's ballet bar dismantled and packed, because it was special to her. It was worn smooth in all the right places! Jenny was sure *that* could not be duplicated in the Colonies. Mirrors, or course, could be purchased and hung after the family arrived.

"What if the house doesn't have room for a ballet studio?" Jenny asked, worried.

"It is a cottage, but there are twelve rooms, plus an attic and a carriage house," Millicent replied. "Surely one of them could be used for dancing."

Jenny was surprised. "You already know about the house? When did you find out? Tell me!"

Millicent smiled. "We got word this morning. It is a lovely place and fairly new. The owners have been using it as a winter home, but they will be visiting family in Europe this year, perhaps indefinitely. They are willing to lease it to a good family who will take care of it, until such time as they decide whether to sell."

"Your father says it is in a residential area near the center of town, not five blocks from the county court house," Violet added. "And a new opera house opened just a few years ago."

"An opera house!"

"Yes, dear, but it is all quite different from London. Not nearly as splendid," Millicent said. "I'm told that things move slowly and quietly in the southern Colonies, especially in small towns. And

79

that—slowly and quietly—will be very good for my health," she added unashamedly. She was playing her role well.

That night Violet slipped a sealed envelope under Jenny's door. Tyler Fleming had led Violet to believe it was a letter of farewell, perhaps declaring his loyalty to Jenny. Actually, it was a short note in his handwriting, which Jenny never told anyone about:

Urgent! I must see you. Same day, same time, same place.

Jenny burned the message into her heart, then burned it with her candle. Three more days until Thursday. Three more nights until midnight. In the rose garden. She could hardly wait!

~~~

Evelyn stopped by with a box of colorful ribbons. "A *bon voyage* gift," she said, handing it to Jenny. "One to match each of your new outfits. Honestly, I cannot imagine anything more exciting than going to the Colonies! I wish I were going. It is simply *marvelous!*"

"Thank you, Evelyn. The ribbons are lovely. You are a dear friend," she added, hugging her. Jenny was excited, too, but she also carried the burden of leaving everything that was dear to her, including Tyler, and that tempered her excitement somewhat. Their secret meeting in the rose garden that night would be very difficult. How could she possibly say good-bye?

"So you leave Monday morning, just a few more days. Have you finished packing?"

"Almost." Jenny stood quietly in the center of the room for a few seconds, then suddenly burst into tears and flung herself across the bed.

"Jenny! Whatever is the matter? I thought you were happy about going." Evelyn sat beside her. "Oh … of course. You don't want to leave Tyler. I understand. Please, dear, don't cry. I am going to clear the way for both of you, remember? I am going to take care of that little problem with Angus while you're gone. Why, when I get finished, Ada Gregory will have him eating out of her glove like a horse eats oats! Now there's a picture for you. More than a little resemblance, wouldn't you say?"

Jenny couldn't help laughing through her tears. "Oh, Evelyn, it's not that," she said, sitting up. "Of course I shall miss Tyler, but it just occurred to me how much ... how much I shall miss *you*, my very best friend ever."

Evelyn blinked back a tear of her own and hugged Jenny. She couldn't possibly cry and be an adult at the same time. "I shall write often," she said, "and you do the same. Time will pass quickly enough, you'll see. Six months is not so very long, after all."

It was an eternity.

Chapter 9

Her father had already gone to bed when Jenny slipped down the back stairs. He seemed more contented these days, less driven. He, too, was looking forward to the extended vacation he would have while Millicent "took her cure." He slept very soundly lately. Jenny thought of that as she closed the outside door and moved into the shadows, but from then on her thoughts were only of Tyler. Her love. Light and quick as a butterfly, she moved through the statuary, through the gate to the rose garden, and into his waiting arms.

"Oh, my darling, I thought tonight would never come!" he said between kisses. "I have missed you terribly."

"I've missed you, too, Tyler. Your message said 'urgent.' Has something happened?"

"Of course it's urgent. And something has very definitely happened—you are leaving on Monday! This is the last time we can be together. The *only* time."

Jenny melted into his arms once again. And he did not waste any time touching her breasts. It was a lovely night, not even the usual mist, and he pulled her to the ground to sit beneath a small maple tree. Jenny felt warmly comforted by the tree's branches, the security of the stone wall, and the heady scent of roses.

He held her and kissed her, and did those wonderful things with his tongue, weakening her with pleasure. Then he leaned against the

82

tree and gently placed her head on his chest. At the same time he cupped her breasts in his hands.

"We have to talk," he said, his voice husky.

"I-I know," she replied. "But you are making it very difficult to concentrate." All she could think about was the slow movement of his hands, back and forth, back and forth.

"Six months is a long time, and I cannot possibly make the journey over there to see you," he said.

"I didn't expect you to. But you can write. Every day, if you like. And I shall answer every letter. I promise." Then she remembered something. "Tyler, your visit with my father. Please tell me about it. What did he say?"

Tyler shrugged. "It was baffling. He was exceedingly nice, not at all what I had expected. I explained that we were in love, and that I wanted to court you properly. I also told him that I had graduated Oxford and that my prospects were good, though I would never be rich. He seemed very sympathetic."

"And?" Tyler's hands were still moving and Jenny's interest in the conversation was ebbing.

"He said that he had nothing against me personally, but that the time was not right. If I would wait a year, he would be happy to consider my request."

"In a year's time he hopes to have me married off to Angus Newton!"

"I know. Still, it was impossible for me to fault his technique. He even offered me a brandy, which I politely declined."

"Well, I have plans for Angus Newton," Jenny said. And she told him about Ada Gregory. "I have great faith in Evelyn's wiles, too. She will manage it, you'll see."

Tyler chuckled and kissed Jenny again. This time his hand slipped into the neckline of her dress, beneath the fabric and directly onto the soft, eager mound that awaited him. Jenny gasped, but he continued to cover her mouth with kisses, lowering her entire body to the ground. Very slowly he kissed, and probed, and teased, and touched … until Jenny began to relax.

The grass was warm, Tyler was warm, and she was getting *very* warm. His lips moved to her throat, lingering, and then to the tops of her breasts. Involuntarily, she tried to stop him.

"Oh, Jenny, please," he groaned, as he started to unbutton her bodice. She stiffened. "Relax, darling," he said. "I love you. I want to show you how much." She was frightened, but she trusted Tyler, and she let him continue. When her lovely, small breasts were exposed to the night air, she shivered ... but it was nothing like the sensation that bolted through her body when he kissed her erect tips.

"Tyler!" she cried, pulling his head tightly to herself. But he kept kissing, flicking his tongue lightly across her vulnerable skin. Again, she relaxed, surprised to find that she enjoyed the tiny shivers that kept her body tingling. As she lay there, Tyler removed his coat, then his shirt. Jenny quickly averted her eyes.

"Don't be embarrassed, darling," he said. "Look at me. Now touch me. Touch my chest."

She did as he said, hesitantly at first, then with great pleasure, as the curly strands of hair slid through her fingers. Slowly, her hand moved back and forth. Suddenly, her eyes widened in surprise. "Why, yours are ... "

"Yes," he said, smiling. "Mine are hard, too, just like yours. It's natural."

"It is?"

"This is part of what love is—trusting, sharing, touching, and not being embarrassed about it. It is beautiful. You are beautiful." And he kissed her again, very tenderly this time. Jenny felt as if she were melting away.

Then Tyler's hand moved down, over her skirt, and began inching the fabric upward. Her ankles were exposed, then her knees! She stiffened once again.

"Don't be afraid, darling," he said. "Remember that I love you. I want to love every part of you."

She tried to relax, but it was most difficult with his hand on her thigh! Still, she didn't want him to stop. It was something she couldn't explain, even to herself. His mouth was nearly covering her breast now, and his hand was ... oh, dear! It was beneath her underclothing and moving toward ... She stiffened again.

"I love you," he whispered.

She never dreamed he would want to touch her *there*! For heaven's sake, *why*? His hand wasn't moving, but it generated an enormous amount of heat—wonderful, relaxing heat—and Jenny basked in its tenderness. It seemed she had a lot to learn about love.

They lay like that for several moments, merging their senses, breathing the rose-scented air ... and then Tyler's fingers began to move once again, into the most private part of Jenny's body. She reacted at once.

"No, Jenny, my love," he whispered. "Don't squeeze your limbs together. Do just the opposite. You will like it, I promise."

Something in the far recesses of her mind told her this was wrong, but she could not help herself. Tyler's presence was just too powerful. She did as he said, trying to relax as his fingers moved, sliding slowly and tenderly over her moist, innermost parts. He was right—she did like it. She felt warm and fuzzy all over, and sometimes, when he touched a certain place, a tiny *marvelous* shiver would overtake her. His fingers still moving, he kissed her lips, tasting her sweetness; and something even deeper began to stir within her. His fingers moved faster, more urgently, and she found herself clinging tightly to him, moving with the rhythm of his hand, until suddenly her body shook with ... yes, a *spasm* more incredibly wonderful than anything she could ever have imagined! She tried to scream aloud in joy, but Tyler kept his mouth clamped onto hers, engulfing her entire body. When she finally relaxed and began breathing more slowly, he released the kiss.

"I did not want your father to hear that," he said, grinning. She could see him very clearly in the moonlight, looking almost devilish.

"Oh, Tyler," she said, still gasping for breath. Her eyes were shining with joy. "I had no idea ..."

"You still don't, my darling," he said. And he removed her clothes ... all of them. And his clothes ... all of them.

And he introduced her to the rest of the pleasures of love.

~~~

Andrea closed the diary, gasping a little herself. Jenny Alcott had been quite explicit for a young Victorian! Then she felt a little ashamed. Jenny had never intended for anyone else to read what she had written. It was very personal.

Andrea leaned back in her chair and put the diary on the side table. Personal or not, she would begin reading the second one in the morning. As she thought about Tyler Fleming, she still didn't like him very much. He was too smooth, too polished. Not at all like the fumbling, yet kind and gentle Roger Overby had been. Nor was Andrea like Jenny in that respect. Andrea had known exactly what she was getting into. Welcomed it, even. The only thing she hadn't counted on was the consequence. It wasn't that she'd thought it *couldn't* happen to her; it was just that she didn't think about it at all. When she found out, Roger had already been in Paris for two weeks. She wouldn't have bothered him anyway; it was her problem, she'd thought, really believing it at the time. Besides, she didn't love Roger. She knew in her heart that someday, somewhere, she would fall deeply in love with someone. She had an enormous capacity for love, and she knew it was out there, waiting for her. That was what she wanted, not Roger.

And that was what she'd found, years later, when Alex Ferris had lifted her heart and soul clear to heaven and back! He was her Prince Charming, her Knight in Shining Armor, her business partner, her friend, her lover—everything she could ever want in a man.

She was glad she'd never told Roger about the baby ... but neither had she told Alex. Had she protected him by keeping silent? Or had she betrayed him? She loved him too much to hurt him. Ever. Maybe the only one she had really protected *and* betrayed was herself. And right now she was the one who was hurting.

Refusing to let tears form, Andrea rose and walked slowly through the big house, turning out lights. She made sure the doors were locked and bolted, then climbed the stairs, pausing for a moment in the spacious, upper hallway. Which bedroom had been Jenny's? Surely not the huge one she and Alex now occupied. That would have been reserved for Barclay and Millicent Alcott. It was clear now that Jenny had not come here with Tyler. She had come with her parents and her Aunt Violet.

Andrea's appreciation for the endurance of old houses was growing. More than a hundred years had passed since Jenny had arrived, perhaps standing in this very spot to choose her room. What tales the walls could tell, if only they could talk! Andrea felt a little privileged—she was hearing one of the tales directly from the woman who'd lived it. These people, whom she was coming to know as well as she knew her own family, had walked the same halls, touched the same walls, turned the same doorknobs.

She went into her room, put on her nightgown and snuggled beneath the covers, thinking how nice it was to relax in a comfortable bed, even a half-empty one. Then she thought about the old four-poster in the corner guest room, the bed that had been in the house when she and Alex moved in, the bed that made the curtains move. Could it have been in the house when Jenny lived here? It was certainly old enough. Had it belonged to her? Or to Aunt Violet?

After a while Andrea drifted off to sleep. But by then her thoughts were no longer rooted in the past. They had blended into the present, centering on her beloved Alex. She wanted him to come home. She wanted to brush her fingers across the hairs of his chest … and she wanted him to do all the wonderful things with her that Tyler had done with Jenny.

Chapter 10

Alex woke up Saturday morning with a hangover, ordered a quart of orange juice from room service and drank it, and promptly went back to sleep. He hadn't realized he'd had so much to drink the night before, but then, he had been out of the habit since the downshift. Not that he ever was much of a drinker. Just a beer now and then, or wine with a meal. But he and Doug and Shekhey had had before-dinner drinks, during-dinner drinks, and after-dinner drinks; and, as it turned out, he really did get sick. No lie.

Now there was pounding at his door. Or was it in his head? He rolled over and groaned and took a deep breath, but the pounding continued. It was at the door. *Maybe if I ignore it, it'll go away.* He pulled the covers over his head.

"C'mon, Alex, open up! I know you're in there." The pounding continued.

Huh? It was a woman's voice. Had he missed the 10 a.m. meeting? Was he late? He forced himself out of bed, dragging the sheet behind him. With his face against the door he called, "What is it? I'm running late."

"You sure are," she answered. "It's eight o'clock. Open the door."

Eight o'clock? What kind of maniac was this? He'd thought it was much later. "Who is it?" he yelled.

"Just open the door. You'll be glad you did."

He really wasn't in the mood for this. His head still hurt like hell.

"Can't open the door. I'm not dressed."

"Doesn't matter. I've brought some things to make you feel better."

Alex released the chain and pulled the door open just a crack. "Oh, my God," he said under his breath. It was Charlotte! He would have shut the door, but her hand was already in the way.

"Don't panic, honey," she said. "I'm only here to help you."

"Yeah, sure. How did you find me?"

"Doug called. He said he'd been trying to call you but you wouldn't answer your phone. He was worried. He said since you and I'd had such a good time last night, why didn't I come over here and fix you up? You see, I didn't tell him that we hadn't ... well, that the evening ended before it hardly got started."

"Well, we're not going to finish it this morning."

"I know," she said. She pushed the door open. "I really am here to help you." She marched across the room and put a bag of goodies on the bedside table.

Exasperated, Alex threw an arm in the air and slammed the door, still clutching his sheet. "What the hell are you talking about?"

"Hot coffee, lots of it," she said, pulling containers out of the bag. "And aspirin. Also lotion. I'm going to give you a good rub."

"You did all your rubbing last night, Charlotte."

"Not that, silly. I mean your back, shoulders, head—the parts that hurt. I know you're hurting. You're not used to drinking."

"You seem to know a lot about me, and, gee, we've known each other such a short time."

"Don't be sarcastic. It's not *you* I know a lot about. It's *men*. In some ways you're all alike. Sit down and drink this." She handed him a container of hot, black coffee, and he sat on the edge of the bed.

She was dressed conservatively this morning—navy slacks and a silk blouse. Her short dark hair looked freshly washed, and her make-up was almost nonexistent. He couldn't help thinking how much prettier she looked.

"What do you do for a living?" he asked. "I mean other than ... uh, ... "

She laughed, showing a lovely wide smile and beautiful white teeth. "You mean my day job? I'm a lawyer," she said.

"Right."

"It's true. I'm one of a whole string of subordinates in an enormous law firm. Actually, that's where I met Doug. Big pond, little fish. Regular hours, decent pay. Boring job."

Alex stared. "You're … you're a *lawyer* and you—" He took a big gulp of his coffee. "*Why*, for God's sake?"

"I just said it. Boring job."

"But today—"

"Today is Saturday. My time is my own."

"I suppose Doug paid you for this."

"Of course."

He drank his coffee and took the aspirin while Charlotte watched. To her credit, she didn't talk. After a few moments he began to feel better, was actually glad she had come. Now, if she would just go.

"Thanks," he said. "I'm fine now, and I appreciate your visit." Still wrapped in the sheet, he stretched out on his stomach and buried his face in the pillow. The bed was firm but comfortable. "You can go now," he mumbled.

"Oh no, you don't," she said. "This rub is paid for and you're going to get it."

Before Alex could move, she jerked the sheet away and threw it across the room. "I admire a man who sleeps in his skin," she said, slapping cold lotion onto his bare back. He yelled.

Immediately, she began to massage. Alex wanted her to quit … but, dammit! It felt good. She kneaded his back, his sore neck, his aching muscles, his legs and his feet. And she didn't get funny. He was almost asleep.…

"Roll over," she said. "I have to do the other side."

"Go away."

"I'm serious. Don't you feel better now?"

"Yes."

"Well, you'll be even better when I finish. Now roll over."

"Get the sheet."

"And spoil the view?"

"Forget it."

"Look you don't have to worry. You're not getting anything more than was paid for. I'm a businesswoman. A professional. And you don't have anything I haven't seen before. Now roll over."

So he did. And she massaged his chest, his neck, his arms, his stomach and hips. He closed his eyes tightly and tried to relax. Couldn't believe himself—a forty-four-year-old man who'd been around the world and back ... and he was embarrassed!

"It's okay," she said. "I didn't even notice."

At that he had to laugh.

Charlotte began to work on his legs. "Like I said, you only get what's paid for."

Just then the phone rang. Alex groped for the receiver and pulled himself up against the pillows, motioning for Charlotte to get the sheet. Instead, she sat in the chair beside the bed, smiling.

"Hello! Are you there, Alex?"

"Andrea?" Alex gulped, and his body turned bright red all over. It was the first time in his life he could remember blushing. Like a damned teenager! And Charlotte was grinning.

"Alex? Did I wake you?"

"No! I, uh, I ... overslept. But I was up."

Charlotte nodded, pointing strategically.

He grabbed the extra pillow to cover himself and motioned for her to leave. "Glad you called, honey," he said into the phone.

"You sound funny. What are you doing?"

"Wh-what am I doing?"

Charlotte clapped a hand over her mouth.

"I, uh ... I had a little too much to drink last night, and I'm fighting a hangover. Sorry." He covered the receiver and hissed at Charlotte, "Leave *now*. Please!"

"Actually, I'm glad I caught you there," Andrea said. "I wanted to ask you about the flower bulbs you promised Mr. Pinckney for his daughter. He was just here and said she'd be visiting today. I didn't know what to give him."

Charlotte rose. She was a lady, after all. Besides, she'd completed her job. She'd made that clear. So she picked up her purse, winked at him and left. Unfortunately, the heavy door slammed behind her.

Alex yelped.

"What was that?"

"Oh, nothing! I was just ... clearing my throat." Alex relaxed a little, but his mind and body were still confused, and the conversation seemed strained, even to him. He talked with Andrea about the bulbs he'd rooted, and Mr. Pinckney, and lots of other things, including how much he loved her and missed her. Still, he found it difficult to concentrate. When he finally replaced the receiver, he sat on the side of the bed feeling like a fink. That was *Andrea*, and there he'd lain on the bed, naked ... with a woman in the room!

Had she suspected? She hadn't sounded like herself, but neither had he. Would this be something she'd ask him about when he got home? Could he be absolutely honest and tell her what really happened? No, he would take some "space" for himself and forget the whole damned thing!

~~~

Andrea located the bulbs in the potting shed, so she could direct Mr. Pinckney to them later in the day. She was glad she'd been able to get Alex on the phone, but sorry he'd had such a bad morning. It wasn't like him to drink a lot. He'd sounded terrible at first, like he'd wished she hadn't called. But later he talked more like the old Alex. Maybe the hangover was wearing off.

Anyway, he'd be home that night. Everything would be better when she could see his face, look into his eyes. She hoped he would tell her if something was wrong.

Shrugging it off, she went back to the kitchen where she'd been sitting at the bar before Mr. Pinckney had stopped by. She opened Jenny's second book and glanced at the clock. Alex would be home in a little more than ten hours. That seemed like a long time, but she knew she would need every bit of it to finish the last two diaries.

Now, as she began to read, she was surprised to find that a great deal of time had elapsed since Jenny had completed the first one.

> *Dear Diary,*
> *I regret not being able to record the details of our ocean voyage, but truly it was unremarkable. Aunt Violet was seasick the entire time, and I had to attend her—Father certainly couldn't, and it was beyond Mother's capabilities. At home, that sort of thing is left to servants. Suffice it to say, I love my aunt dearly, and I am glad that I was able to help her and give her comfort. Now we are settled in this quiet little town in Georgia, in the most charming cottage one could ever imagine. It has a huge front porch with intricate woodwork all around— they call it "gingerbread" here. There is a pretty picket fence along the sidewalk, and huge oak trees reach out across Dawson Street. There's not a scene in London quite like it. I have chosen the little, center-front bedroom for my own. It suits me. At this moment I am sitting up in bed, in the loveliest four-poster I have ever seen. It is made of walnut wood and has pineapples carved into the tops of each post! ...*

~~~

Andrea took a deep breath. The "little bedroom" Jenny spoke of was the one she now used for painting—her art studio—and the bed was the very one now sitting in her guest room, the bed that had been in the house "for at least seventy-five years," according to her aunt. *You were wrong,* she thought. *It's been here for at least one hundred years!* Why did superstition dictate leaving the bed in the house? Andrea would have to find out. Maybe Jenny would give her a clue.

She was getting that funny feeling again, the strangeness of being "at home," of being inside Jenny's skin. It was almost as if she knew each thing that would happen to Jenny just seconds before she read it in the diary. She didn't, of course. It just seemed that way.

Chapter 11

With the long voyage, Violet's illness, and unpacking and settling in, Jenny had not had much time to think about what had happened between Tyler and her. Now, alone in her new bedroom, she gave it a great deal of thought.

For certain, she had discovered what it was that married people did. But she would never tell Evelyn; she just *couldn't*. It was too embarrassing. She also was certain her own parents had never done it. She could not imagine their doing anything more than sharing a room. As far as she knew, they'd never even kissed, for heaven's sake! It was probably wrong to do it when you weren't married, and that worried her, for she was truly bewildered about her own behavior. It was as if she'd had no control over her senses or her body. Like a volcano readying to erupt, there was no stopping it. Evelyn had been right about one thing—if she liked having her breasts touched, she would surely like *that*! Ladies were not supposed to like it. That much she'd heard from whisperings. Now Jenny knew what *it* was, and she did like it. Did that make her a bad person? How could something that felt so good be bad?

She not only worried about it, she also tried praying about it, but she wasn't very good at praying. Her parents were not "pray-ers," and she hadn't had much practice. They were all going to be praying soon, though. On Sunday, in fact, because their neighbor, Mrs.

Cathcart, had said to Millicent, "Everyone who is anyone goes to church. It's the place to meet all the right kind of people." That was good enough for Millicent Alcott. The whole family would attend the Methodist Episcopal Church, just two blocks from their home.

"It is the best choice for your family," Mrs. Cathcart said, "because it is closest in practice to the Church of England." She ought to know, she said, since she had traveled extensively. Jenny had listened to her boring travel tales over endless cups of weak tea. "Of course there's a Baptist church nearby, too," Mrs. Cathcart said, pronouncing it Babdis, "but I don't believe you would be happy there."

It didn't make one whit of difference to Jenny. She did not know what a Babdis was anyway.

~~~

Becca Weaver moved in the next day, into the furnished room over the carriage house. Jenny was fascinated with Becca, first because she had never seen a colored person up close, at least not to talk to, then because Becca talked so differently—even different from her mother's new friends, whose drawling speech was a trial to understand! Jenny had to ask Becca over and over again what she said. Becca didn't mind at all. Her eyes twinkled, and it seemed that when she laughed, her whole body shook, its parts moving separately. She had the prettiest white teeth Jenny had ever seen.

"Law, chile," she said, "if you think I talks funny, you should hear yo'self, goin' on with words I never heard spoke, like 'amiss,' and 'singular,' and 'scones'!" Her eyes got real big. "Just you wait 'til you tastes my biscuits, you won't want no more o' them dried up things." She pointed to Jenny's scone-making efforts in a basket on the table.

"They're not dried up. I just didn't make them right."

"Hmmph!"

Jenny laughed. She couldn't wait to taste Becca's biscuits. And get some cooking lessons, too. Jenny loved to cook, or at least to try. Millicent had hired Becca to be a combination cook and maid, and her son, Young Moses, would come for a few hours each day to take care of the yard and do minor chores. Millicent had been at a loss for household help until her neighbors offered to assist her in finding someone. Like Jenny, she had not been around colored people very much, but the ladies insisted that was the thing to do. "Everyone has Negroes," Mrs. Cathcart had said.

"Young Moses still lives on the plantation," Becca explained, "with his father, Ol' Moses. I calls my husband 'Holy Moses' myself, he's so strict religious!" She chuckled. "We never did get along too good, and workin' for yo' folks seemed like the answer to our troubles."

Young Moses, with Violet's and Jenny's help, assembled Jenny's ballet bar and attached it to the wall of her new attic studio, even though he said good-naturedly, "Cain't figure why you'd want a railin' where there ain't no stairs." When he left with his tools, he was grinning and shaking his head. Jenny heard him mumble, "White fo'ks!"

"It's perfect," Jenny said to Violet. "I like it even better than my room in London."

"Are you sure? It seems a bit isolated to me, all the way at the top of the house. Why, when you look out the window, you're eye-to-eye with treetops!"

"That is what makes it special," Jenny replied. "I have an entire floor to myself."

Violet laughed. "You can count on that, since getting up here is no easy task."

"You mean setting out the little stair-box? That's no problem." She turned her attention elsewhere. "Just look at the floor, Aunt Violet, how pretty it is." Violet would have preferred it with some shine, but she knew what Jenny meant—it was just right for dancing. The boards were smooth and straight and tight, but not slippery. "Young Moses will hang the mirrors tomorrow," Jenny said, "then it will be finished."

"Except for one thing."

"What is that?"

"My chair." Violet smiled, chiding her. "You didn't think the inaccessibility of your little hideaway would keep *me* out, did you?"

"Oh, Aunt Violet!" Jenny squeezed her aunt's hand. "You know I'd never want to keep you away. We shall bring up that lovely bentwood rocker that's stored in the trunk room. It's perfect. You can sit in it and rock, and crochet, and watch me dance."

"And listen to your prattle."

"Do I go on so?"

"Sometimes, but I always find it interesting."

"Come here," Jenny said, pulling her toward the window. "I'll show you something *very* interesting." She knelt down on the floor and removed the short board nearest the sill. "See? It's a secret place. I can keep things in it!"

Violet knelt, too. "However did you find it?"

"I stepped on it and it didn't feel right." She lifted out a tiny box. "Someone else used it for secrets, too. Look." She removed the lid, allowing Violet to look inside. There was one dried rose, nothing else. "A red rose, you know, is a declaration of love," Jenny said, holding the box out to catch more of the window light. "Isn't it romantic?"

"I suppose so. Or sad. It could mean anything."

"I choose to think it was given to a young lady by someone she loved, and she saved it to remind her of him. I am going to leave it here. Maybe she will come back for it one day." She put the box back in its resting place, then looked out the window, a sudden sadness overtaking her features.

"Jenny, is something wrong?"

Jenny bit her lip, then replied, "I don't have anything to remind me of Tyler, except the first letter he wrote me, back in England. He never gave me anything."

"Well … there wasn't much time actually. And, too, he did not have a great deal of money."

"He gave you violets," Jenny said, tears forming.

"Oh, darling, that was just a joke! You know that."

"I know. But he could have given me one. Just one." She sounded like a petulant child.

"You're worried now because you have been apart so long. I am sure you'll feel much better when you receive his first letter from across the ocean." Violet stood. "Let's go downstairs now. Becca has biscuits and honey for us."

"Aunt Violet," Jenny said, as Violet preceded her down the attic stairs, "shouldn't a letter have arrived by now?"

Violet didn't answer. Jenny was sure that she had pretended not to hear.

~~~

That Sunday the Alcott family attended church with the Methodists. Since it was only two blocks away and the sun was shining, they walked, presenting a perfect picture of up-to-date finery and fashion to those who passed by in carriages. Becca had had to let out the waist of Jenny's favorite Sunday dress. She had refused to wear all those bones and straps and stays and laces, because, as she had said, "Everything is too tight and uncomfortable in this heat!"

As they approached the church, Violet said, "These people certainly do not spare expense on their houses of worship, for such a small town, I mean."

"The building is new, Violet," Barclay said. "It's only been here— let's see, built in 1885 according to Sheriff Doss—seven years; so of course it still looks fine."

They had been used to the cathedrals in London; and, even though they had seen the imposing Methodist structure many times at a distance, its size and beauty were not actually apparent until they stood on the steps. There were many shades of brick laid in intricate designs, and beautiful stained glass windows that drew attention upward to the heaven-bound steeple. It was nice. Not ornate, but tasteful and inviting.

"I believe we could feel at home here," Millicent said.

At the top of the steps they were greeted by a familiar face, Mr. J.L. Pringle—they had visited his grocery store on Broad Street just the day before. He handed them hymnals and fans and called them by name, which impressed Barclay Alcott no end.

The inside of the church was very pretty and comfortably appointed, though Jenny was quick to notice the inevitable spittoons—a couple of dozen of them scattered throughout. She could not imagine why men had to adopt that nasty habit.

Following the singing of "Amazing Grace," the family listened politely to Pastor Wynn's sermon, which Jenny feared would go on until nightfall. Actually, it was during the sermon that she finally prayed, trying to find out if she were a bad person for doing what she did with Tyler.

She did not get an answer, but she did feel a sense of comfort and decided that had been worth enduring the sermon.

~~~

"How does God answer prayer?" she asked Becca the next afternoon. They were sitting on the back porch, shelling peas.

"Well, now," Becca said. "They's many ways. Sometimes you wakes up in the mornin' jes' knowin' the answer, like a bright light suddenly fills up yo' head. Then they's the 'still, small voice.' That's when it comes over you gradual-like. And sometimes He jes' works it out, puttin' things in yo' path until you gets the idea that you s'pose to—or you not s'pose to—do whatever it is you prayin' about."

"Doesn't He ever just speak plainly?"

Becca chuckled. "Not often, chile. You prayin' about something 'portant these days?"

"No ... well, yes. At least it is important to me."

"That's all that counts. If it's 'portant to you, it's 'portant to God."

"But I prayed yesterday, and He still hasn't answered."

"Did you pray fo' patience?"

Jenny tossed her handful of peas back into the bowl. "Oh, honestly, Becca, you sound just like Mother and Aunt Violet—patience, patience, patience!"

"I gather you didn't pray for it. You sho' don't have any. Somethin' botherin' you, chile? Somethin' ol' Becca can help you with?"

"No! I mean, it's personal."

"I see." She gave Jenny another handful of peas. "Well, if it gets too much to bear, an' you need someone to talk with—other than God Hisself, o' course—you just remember Becca's got open ears and a closed mouth. I'll do my best, chile."

" … Thank you," Jenny whispered. She would remember that. More and more she liked to spend time with Becca, because Becca was … well, *real*. There was no "keeping up appearances" with Becca, or with Young Moses for that matter. With both of them, what you saw was exactly what there was, and what they said was exactly what they meant. Like the time Becca told Millicent to stay out of "her" kitchen. She was kind, but firm.

"Miz Alcott," she had said, "you a nice lady, sho'nuff. But you cain't cook and you sho' don't know nothin' about the stuff that grows in gardens around here. You jes' leave things to ol' Becca and you'll be happy. I promise." Oddly, Millicent was happy.

And then there was the time Young Moses said to Jenny that Mrs. Cathcart walked like she had a broom handle shoved up her nose. Jenny had giggled herself silly.

But even more remarkable was the day they were making apple pie together and Becca said that Holy Moses believed "spare the rod and spoil the child" extended to his wife.

"You mean he *hit* you?" Jenny had asked.

"Hit me more'n once, chile."

"What did you do?"

"After 'nuff times I moved out. That's why I'm here."

"And Young Moses?"

"Oh, he's big now an' he stands up to his daddy. They can fight it out an' call it exercise. Me, I yelled back plenty, but the more I yelled the madder he got." She lowered her voice. "I jes' don't believe the man o' the house has to be *that* much of a boss-man, no matter what the Good Book says."

Jenny's father was certainly a "boss-man," but he had never, *ever* hit anyone. Jenny believed Becca's story, but she was surprised that Becca had told her. In her world, people didn't even mention such things. Jenny had been stuffed chock-full of pretension and propriety from the time she was a little girl. She'd always followed the rules … except for what happened with Tyler Fleming. And *that* worried her so much lately that she felt her very soul was being eaten away! And *why* hadn't he written?

~~~

On Wednesday the letter arrived. Jenny snatched it from Violet's hands and scampered to the attic.

Jenny's Four-Poster

Chapter 12

The letter was not inside the diary. Andrea looked for it, very carefully turning the next few pages. Nor did Jenny refer to it in her next lines.

Andrea pushed herself away from the bar and put her dishes in the sink. Her back ached from sitting so long on the bar stool, so she stretched every muscle she thought she had. Still, it wasn't enough. Sometimes, like now, she wished she could shake all over, like a dog does. *What a great feeling that must be*, she thought.

She went upstairs to the slant-ceilinged bathroom, which in Jenny's day had been the "trunk room," and splashed cold water on her face. Then she went to the corner guest room and sat on Jenny's bed, running her hands up the smooth wood of the posts, sliding her fingers over and around the carved pineapples.

"Jenny, my girl," she said aloud, "as soon as I get my art studio moved to the attic, your bed is going back into your little bedroom! I'll put a lovely patchwork quilt on it, and I'll repaper the walls with something you would have liked, something with flowers, maybe tiny roses." The curtain on one of the closed front windows fluttered briefly. It startled Andrea. She listened carefully for the air-conditioning. It was not running, nor did it start up in the next few seconds. *That's funny*, she thought. *Last time it was the curtain in my studio that moved.*

"See those things, Jenny?" she said more quietly, glancing toward the walnut-framed mirror across the room and the padded heart-back chair in the corner. She kept an eye on the curtain. "They'll be just right for your room. The only other item we need is a wardrobe. I'll hit the antiques stores first thing next week. I promise!" Warily, she turned her full attention to the curtain ... but this time it didn't move.

Andrea relaxed with a sudden realization. She certainly felt Jenny's presence in the house. She was sure now that was what it was—not *déjà vu*, but a faint sense of "being" that seemed to come and go. Perhaps her state of mind, her confusion and uncertainty about life, had made her receptive to Jenny's spirit. Was there something Jenny wanted? Something Andrea could do for her? Restoring Jenny's bedroom would be as much fun as turning her dance studio into an art studio, she thought. Maybe, in the process, Andrea would find herself restored as well.

Suddenly, she remembered what Jenny had shown her Aunt Violet. She hurried to the attic door, pulled out the stepstool, and climbed the stairs. Sunshine streamed through the big front window, and Andrea quickly sat on the floor in the midst of it, peering into the space that had been Jenny's "secret place." Would the surprise still be there? Jenny had said she would leave it.

Andrea couldn't see anything, but she put her hand in and stretched her fingers under the floorboards, reaching in all directions. Sure enough, she touched something smooth and hard. Carefully, she pulled it out—a small, fragile, cloisonné box. Her hands shook a little as she tried to lift the lid. It was stuck, and there wasn't a thing in the clean-swept attic to pry it with.

She took the box down to her art studio and sat at her drawing table, picking up a sharp knife. Very carefully, she loosened the lid all the way around, then pried it up. Inside was a dried rose, just as Jenny had said! She didn't touch it, because it looked as though it might disintegrate in an instant, but she stared at it for a long time. Jenny had written in her diary, "A declaration of love. Perhaps she will return for it one day." It had been more than a hundred years. Had Jenny been writing about Andrea Ferris?

Alex had given her red roses off and on over the years. She still had one of them—a very special one, the one he had given her the night he'd proposed. It was pressed between the pages of her favorite book of poems. In fact, it was pressed right into the middle of "How do I love thee? Let me count the ways ..." Elizabeth Barrett Browning. Written long before Jenny was born, but still the most beautiful love poem Andrea had ever known. It expressed, more perfectly than she ever could, the way she felt about Alex, the way she would always feel about him.

" ... to the depth and breadth and height my soul can reach / to the level of every day's most quiet need / freely / purely / with the breath, smiles, tears, of all my life!"

After they had known each other a year, she illustrated that poem on canvas and gave it to Alex without telling him what it represented. He'd always kept it on his office wall in Atlanta; now it hung in his little office in downtown Thomasville.

"Such beautiful color," he had said as he unwrapped it. Then he looked at her very tenderly. "From blazing passion to soft, warm, and cuddly." She was embarrassed. He was more perceptive than she'd imagined. "Oh, don't look away," he said, turning her chin in his big hand. "I have the same feelings inside of me, feelings for you. I just don't have such a wonderful way of expressing them. Come in here—I want to show you something."

She'd gone to his apartment after work to take him the painting and to take him out for dinner. It was his birthday. He took her hand and led her to the bedroom—she'd been there before—but this time, when he opened the door, candles were glowing by the window. They were on a small table set for two, with china and silver. In the center was a single red rose in a crystal vase.

"What is this?" She was too surprised to say more.

"The caterer will be here in an hour. That gives us time to enjoy a nice, chilled *Beaujolais*. Shall I pour?"

"Alex, this is your birthday. I'm supposed to be treating you!"

"You are," he replied. "Just by being here."

It had been a wonderful evening, the best they had ever had.

They'd dined on *Veal Scaloppine al Limone*, spinach salad, fresh fruit, and *Gruyere* cheese, listened to their favorite old Frank Sinatra tunes, and watched Atlanta's lights twinkle across the skyline. High above the city they danced, made love with their eyes, their words, and finally their bodies.

Toward morning she awakened to find Alex stroking her silky hair, entwining it in his fingers.

"You are the most beautiful creature I have even seen," he said.

She knew she wasn't beautiful, but she loved hearing him say it, knowing he meant it. She smiled and touched his lips.

"Andrea," he said.

"Hmm?"

His voice was soft and husky. "I love you more than I have ever loved anyone or anything in my entire life. I want to spend the rest of my life with you, if you'll have me."

She put her fingers over her own mouth, not believing what she had heard.

"Will you marry me?" he asked. "Please?"

Had they really come this far? To marriage? At this stage in both their lives? How should she answer him? Despite her *cum laude* degree, her hard-won success, her money, the high regard in which she was held by friends and acquaintances, she still had a little girl trapped inside her head—the one who had grown up with feelings of inadequacy and then, later, guilt. So much guilt! She'd turned her back on the narrow way of life, disappointed her mother, had Roger Overby's baby … and couldn't talk about any of it. Would Alex still want to marry her if he knew? Her mother had called her "filthy," and "an abomination unto the Lord."

"Andrea?"

" … Oh, yes!" she cried, burying her face in his chest, lest he see the tears. "I love you, Alex. I love you … love you … love you … "

~~~

Andrea closed the cloisonné box, returning it and its "declaration of love," to its ancient hiding place. Maybe someday she would add her book of poems, containing her own red rose. Maybe a hundred years from now, if the house were still standing, someone would find it.

She went back downstairs, picked up the second diary and settled onto the front porch swing. Even though temperatures remained hot during Southern autumns, her porch was fairly cool because huge live oaks shaded it and breezes swept through it. Andrea shed her sandals, pulled her feet up under her, and let the wind move the swing.

~~~

Two days after Jenny received Tyler's letter, Violet asked her about it. It was early morning, and they were sitting on the fourposter in Jenny's tiny bedroom.

"You've been more low-spirited than ever, Jenny. What's wrong?"

"I don't know. I haven't been feeling well lately."

"I thought Tyler's letter would make you happy. But it did not, did it?"

Jenny closed her eyes tightly against the sting of tears, but she did not reply.

Violet took hold of her hand. "Can't you let me help you, dear?" And Jenny's tears spilled through her lashes.

"It's nothing really. ... I should not be upset. ... I mean, he didn't say anything *bad* or *wrong* ...."

"He didn't say anything at all. Is that it? Not what you expected?"

Jenny nodded. "It was just a plain old letter and a short one at that. No more than I would expect from Evelyn, for heaven's sake!" Angrily, she jabbed at her tears. "I thought he would at least say he *loved* me!"

Violet handed Jenny a clean handkerchief. "Perhaps he is just being cautious."

"But he said it before. He said he loved me. Why can't he write it in a letter?"

"Have you written those words to him?" Jenny nodded again and wiped her eyes. "Well, then," Violet said, "I believe your problem is more embarrassment than devastation. You feel a little embarrassed because you wrote Tyler a love letter and he did not write one back."

"I wrote more than one."

Violet smiled. "That's all right, Jenny. Don't ever be embarrassed or apologetic about feelings. I have told you that before. We all have them. Sometimes we find ourselves in a fine stew because of them, but there is nothing wrong with having feelings. Let's look at it this way. Tyler knows exactly where you stand. Perhaps he is still trying to decide where he stands."

"But he said he loved me. He did! I thought he wanted to marry me."

"Did he say so?"

"Well, no ... but he implied as much."

"Young men often imply more than they intend, Jenny."

"Did your Samuel?" Jenny had spoken sharply, and she clamped her hand over her mouth as soon as the words escaped. "I'm sorry," she said. "That was cruel."

"It's all right." Violet patted Jenny's hand. "You have not been yourself lately. And yes, at first Samuel did imply more than he intended. Later, though, he realized that he truly did want to marry me."

"So you think Tyler just needs more time?"

"I don't know, but I do believe that these months of separation will enable both of you to make intelligent decisions, if you use the time wisely. Let's concentrate on ballet, Jenny—your opportunities are here—and let the problems with Tyler work themselves through in their own time."

Just then there was a knock on the door, and Becca entered with a tray.

"Thought you ladies might enjoy havin' breakfast in here, jes' the two of you. I'll set it on that little table by the window."

"How lovely, Becca," Violet said. "What have you got?"

Becca smiled her big, wide smile as she sashayed across the room.

Error

 107

"Biscuits, o' course, an' oatmeal, some eggs 'n fried pork, and grits with red-eye gravy."

Jenny grabbed the chamber pot and bolted out the door.

"Now what you s'pose the matter with her?" Becca asked, knowingly.

Violet's face suddenly drained of color.

~~~

At first she'd thought it was something she ate or the change in water, but after the second episode she was convinced it was a matter of adjusting to the intense summer heat of the Deep South. Now, as Jenny cleaned herself up for the fourth time, she wondered if she would make it through the six months they were to stay here. *London was never like this*!

After she had rested a few moments, she made her way back to her bedroom. Violet was still there, but Becca and the breakfast (mercifully!) were gone. Wordlessly, Violet helped her into a clean chemise and tucked her into bed.

"Thank you, Aunt Violet," Jenny said. "This makes four mornings in a row now, and I am exhausted. I don't know what has come over me."

Violet sat carefully on the bed and looked lovingly, yet fearfully, at her niece. This would not be an easy task, especially for a maiden lady. *Nevertheless*, she thought, *I must do it, because telling Millicent first is no alternative at all.*

"I am afraid I do know what has come over you, my dear."

"You do? Is it the water? Have you been sick, too?"

"Jenny ... I don't quite know how to approach this, except to be blunt. Were you ... were you intimate with Tyler Fleming?"

Jenny was suddenly wary. "Intimate? What do you mean, intimate?"

"Did he ... touch you in certain places ... in certain ways that might have embarrassed or frightened you?"

Jenny shut her eyes tightly. *Oh, no!* she thought. *I cannot discuss this with Aunt Violet*! She could feel a telltale blush creeping up her neck and into her face.

"How did you know?" she asked, her eyes still shut.

Violet's sigh was deep, almost a moan. There was no doubt about it now. "Morning sickness is a symptom," she said. "Also, Becca's had to let out some of your dresses, not because of the heat, as you suggested, but because you've put on a little weight. That's another symptom."

"A symptom of what I *did*?"

"No, dear. They are symptoms of … well, … of being with child."

Jenny's eyes popped wide open. "Wh-what?"

"You are going to have a baby, Jenny."

Jenny did not say a word, but her heart was pounding so loudly she was sure Violet could hear it. A *baby*? It wasn't possible. She was barely sixteen, and she wasn't even married, for heaven's sake! *But if that's what married people do, then maybe that's how—* Her "Oooh" was nearly inaudible.

"Have you … did you miss your last monthly?"

Jenny nodded. "But I was glad, because it's such a bother anyway. Is that a symptom, too?"

"Yes. Oh, Jenny, whatever possessed you to do it? No, no. Forget I asked. I know exactly what happened. Tyler was a convincing young man and you could not help yourself. Besides, it's too late to worry about why. We need to think about *what*. What to do next."

"Did … did you ever do it, Aunt Violet?" Jenny pulled the sheet up around her mouth as she spoke.

Violet could not help smiling at the impertinence of innocence. "No, dear. But I almost did. I wanted to."

"I didn't know it would make a baby. You mean my parents did *that* …?"

"Yes. It's how you came into the world." Violet stood. "You should have been told. You never should have been left to discover it for yourself. At least I was told by a young married friend. How I despise the archaic practice of leaving instruction to husbands! Look where it gets us. Women—mothers—are not credited for any intelligence whatsoever!" She began to pace. "Jenny, I'm sorry. This is all my fault. I encouraged you to see Tyler. Damn my spinsterish naiveté! If only I had realized what was happening, I could have warned you. I should have taught you, despite convention!"

Tears welled beneath Jenny's eyelids. "Don't blame yourself, Aunt Violet. It was my own fault. I knew it was wrong, but it was so ... exciting. It was wonderful and terrible at the same time. I have even been praying about it because I felt so guilty. And after all that, Tyler didn't write, and then when he did it was ... " The tears spilled over her cheeks. "It was nothing," she whispered.

"There, now." Violet sat back down on the bed, leaned over, and hugged Jenny to herself. She held her until the weeping stopped.

"I guess Tyler gave me something to remember him by, after all," Jenny said quietly. Suddenly she cried aloud, "Oh, no! Everyone will know what I did! If I am going to have a baby, everyone will know I did *that*!" Then she sobbed in earnest.

When she had quieted once again, Violet wiped her face with water from the bedside pitcher. As she did so, Becca knocked and entered with a cup of warm milk.

"Drink this, chile," she said, holding it to Jenny's lips. "'Twill settle yo' stomach."

"We have a problem, Becca" Violet said.

"An' I knows what it is. I helped many a baby into this world, Lord knows, an' I'd be a fool indeed, if I didn' reco'nize the signs."

"Oh, Becca, what are we going to do?" Jenny wailed.

"You gonna tell yo' mama," Becca answered, "an' she gonna have one o' her spells fo' sure, but you still gonna tell her."

~~~

Becca's prediction was an understatement. Millicent collapsed in a full swoon, and Barclay Alcott nearly had apoplexy.

Chapter 13

Jenny could hear them all afternoon, clear across the wide upper hallway, through their closed bedroom door. They were not really arguing, because Millicent never argued, but they were talking rather loudly and slamming doors and drawers as they discussed Jenny's fate.

Barclay first wanted to box Tyler Fleming's ears and string him to a tall pine, then he wanted to force a marriage and turn him into a model son-in-law. The latter was a more attractive option to Millicent, but as soon as she said so, Barclay bellowed that he didn't even *like* the fortune-hunting and something-else-hunting devil!

Jenny's cheeks burned as she listened, but she could not help herself. Surely when they settled down, they would allow her to express her own wishes. She could not imagine forcing Tyler into marriage, but then the whole issue was moot, because Tyler loved her. As soon as he knew about the baby he would hurry to her side. *They ought to know that!*

"But if they don't marry, what will become of the *baby*?" Millicent wailed from across the hall. "We cannot keep it here! What would people *think*?"

"We could bloody well get rid of it before it's even born," Barclay said. This was followed by the loud slamming of a closet door. Jenny was horrified. *Surely he's not suggesting killing my baby!*

"I have an idea, Barclay," Millicent said. "We could leave the baby here when we go back to London. Then we could hasten her marriage to Angus Newton!"

"She is ruined for marriage, Millicent. You know perfectly well no respectable man would have her."

"But Angus won't know, if we never tell him."

"Of course he would *know*, Millicent, unless he's a complete idiot, which I doubt! Actually, Jenny was right when she said Angus is a goose. He is. Nevertheless, he would make a damned fine husband."

Jenny wanted to jump out of bed, storm across the hall, and give them both a piece of her mind. How dare they make decisions for her as if she were an empty-headed doll! Damned fine husband, indeed! How could her father even *consider* her doing *that* with Angus Newton! It made her stomach churn just to think about it!

But she did not confront her parents. Instead, she quickly dressed herself and went downstairs. She wouldn't listen to their nonsense another minute!

For a long time she sat on the front porch swing, thinking about her "situation," as her mother kept referring to it. Other than the fact—and there was no denying it—that everyone in the world would know she had done *that*, what was so terrible about having a baby? Babies were nice things to have, all cuddly and sweet and such good company. She started moving the swing back and forth, back and forth, back and forth. The more she thought about it, the more she liked the idea. The baby could stay with her most of the time, even when she danced in her studio. And she was certain Becca would help. Becca loved babies! And of course Tyler would be thrilled, though she would not be able to join him in London until the baby was strong enough to travel. Perhaps Tyler could come to America for a few weeks—that would be ... well, it would be *marvelous*! She and Tyler and their baby! What would she name it?

"Afternoon, Miss Alcott."

Jenny looked up to see the postman at the fence, unlatching the gate. She jumped up and ran to meet him.

"Mail from London today," he said, holding out two letters. He waited, expecting conversation, which was the Southern way, but Jenny snatched the letters, dismissed him with a quick "thank you" and hurried back to the porch.

One letter was for her father, and the other was for her—from Evelyn! She tore it open. It was full of Evelyn's usual chatter, much of it very amusing, and a little gossip; but the closing paragraph dealt her a devastating blow:

> ... *Jenny, dear, I hate telling you this but I feel I must. I saw Tyler Fleming at the Savoy last evening—with Anne Whitehall! He did not notice me at first, he was so busy fussing over her! They were holding hands and everything! He even kissed her as he held her chair! Oh, Jenny, I wish you were here to keep him in line—he's such a marvelous catch. And I know if he could just see you, he would forget all about Anne. She's a potato compared to you! Well, I walked over to their table and made a point of speaking to him. He received my unspoken message, too, because his face turned scarlet—yes, it did! ...*

Jenny let the letter drop to her lap. Tyler had been kissing another girl? Slow, hot tears filled her eyes and rolled down her face onto the letter, smearing Evelyn's ink. Why would he kiss another girl? *Doesn't he love me anymore? Did he touch Anne Whitehall's breasts? Did he do the other with her, too? What about the baby—his baby? Would he even care?*

She sat there a long time, the swing motionless. And in that time, as her tears of bewilderment dried into tiny crystals of realization, Jenny Alcott changed from a girl to a woman. She made the first decision of her adult life: *Tyler Fleming will never know about the baby, because I will never tell him*!

~~~

After a break to help Mr. Pinckney carry the pots of flower bulbs to his shed, Andrea put Evelyn's letter back into the diary and laid it on the swing beside her. The last page was all Jenny had saved, and it was so old and tear-stained that it was barely readable. Jenny, too, had been sitting on a swing, on the same porch, probably in the same place, when she had read Evelyn's news. Now, a century later, Andrea Ferris was there, feeling Jenny's pain more acutely than she would have imagined possible. When Jenny was happy, Andrea was happy; if Jenny hurt, Andrea hurt; if Jenny cried, Andrea cried. She wasn't sure she liked dredging up all the old pain, both hers and Jenny's, but she could no more walk away from Jenny now than she could walk away from Alex Ferris. Not that she'd ever considered leaving Alex. She only wanted things to be different, a little more like they used to be, not quite so placid.

Last week she had told him she didn't want to sit and watch life go by. She'd been terribly upset. But now, that problem seemed very small. She was thinking about her own baby. Jenny had said she would never tell Tyler about theirs. And Andrea had never told Alex. Of course there was a slight difference—Andrea's baby had not belonged to Alex. Still, should she have told him? Should he know about the traumatic birth, and that it was the reason he and Andrea could never have children?

Why doesn't Alex ever ask questions? Sometimes his attitude frustrated her completely! Yet that was one of the things that had attracted her to him. He was the most secure person she had ever known. He'd had such a "normal" middle-class upbringing—good student, played high school baseball, had lots of friends and a mom who loved to cook for them. Andrea, on the other hand, had always wished she could participate in school activities, but she was never allowed. She didn't even attend her senior prom, because dancing was a "sin." All of that hurt, and she could not see any good reason for it. When she was little, she buried her damaged feelings deep inside; but when she was older, she dug them up and spit them out.

"Doesn't anything ever bother you, Alex?" she asked him once. "That man just criticized your work in front of someone else!"

"That's *his* problem," Alex answered calmly. "My work is good.

People who matter know that." He accepted everyone at face value. And he had accepted Andrea Cooper the same way. Never questioned what she told him, just loved her dearly and believed in her.

What is all of this about? she asked herself, finally. *Is there a reason for finding these diaries? A reason for exposing my nerve endings? We're similar, Jenny. Is that why you've sought me out?*

Andrea was convinced that her being drawn to the house, and now into the lives of a family long gone, was coming from Jenny herself. She'd always thought such inexplicable things were "horsefeathers"—her father's favorite word—but not anymore. She thought of the comparisons in their lives. She'd made the same decisions Jenny had. And why not? She'd been offered the same choices.

"What would people think?" Were attitudes really much different a century later?

Well, yes, they were now, Andrea admitted to herself. Twenty-some years ago, however, when she was pregnant with Roger Overby's baby, her mother's generation was struggling, trying desperately to keep one foot in each century. It had been difficult.

"Andrea, how *could* you?" her mother had asked, bawling all the while. She had just been told about the pregnancy. "You've had a good, Christian upbringing. Your father and I taught you right from wrong. We were very strict about it. And now you've done *this*, of all things! I am glad your father is dead, yes I am. Your sin would have killed him! How could you do this to *me*?"

"I didn't do it to hurt you, Mother," Andrea replied quietly. "It was for me. I had a lovely summer."

"Aaagh! Lovely! What you did was filthy, Andrea Jane. *Filthy*, you hear me?"

"It didn't seem that way."

"What do you know about it? You let that dirty beatnik take advantage of you. He wanted one thing and one thing only, and you were too stupid to realize it. Don't you know all men want the same thing? For a smart girl, you were very stupid! I ought to turn you out of the house and let you dwell in your own sin, but I'll not do that, no I won't. I'll do my Christian duty and see that you're cared for, though it won't be in this house."

"Wh-what do you mean?"

"You'll go to your Aunt Mary in Birmingham. She's worldly and wouldn't think twice about taking you. Not a bit like her brother, your father. Ordinarily, I'd worry about her corrupting you, but the good Lord knows you're corrupted already. An abomination, that's what it is!"

So eighteen-year-old Andrea went to Aunt Mary Cooper's charming little wisteria-covered cottage on the outskirts of Birmingham, leaving her mother home to moan about what a disappointment she had been.

~~~

Jenny Alcott wasn't going to be sent anywhere. She would be a prisoner in her own home. Barclay had decided it, and that was that. He hadn't actually used the word "prisoner," but that was most certainly what she would be.

"You'll not leave the house until after the child is born," he had ordered. "What's more, you shall stay on the upper floors and away from the windows. Your mother and I do not care to have anyone know about your humiliating ... situation. Isn't that right, Millicent?"

"Yes, dear. But Barclay, what will we tell people who ask about her?"

"We shall *lie*, bygod! Do you have a better idea?"

Millicent shuddered. "No, dear," she said.

"Let it be known that Jenny has taken an extended holiday. With Violet, of course."

"What!" Jenny cried. "You're going to make Aunt Violet a prisoner, too?"

"Call it what you will," he answered. "Violet's partly responsible for this smelly kettle of fish. The two of you may keep each other company. Just be glad Fate saw fit to move us out of London in time.

If this became public knowledge there, it would ruin your mother. God knows she doesn't need any more affliction."

"What has this to do with Mother?"

At that, Millicent swooned, and Barclay ordered Jenny to her room.

The next day Becca came up the stairs, dropping her soft, heavy body onto the comfortable chair beside Jenny's bed. "Well, chile," she said with a sigh. "Things could be worse."

"Not much."

"Yes, they could. Here you is in a comf'table house with plenty to eat and good people to look after you. You can spend yo' days readin' an' doin' needlework, an' jes' whatever you wants."

"I want to dance."

"No, ma'am!" Becca sat up straight, her eyes big as turnips. "You don' do no such a thing! You gonna take care o' yo'self an' have the healthiest, prettiest baby ever born. Why, I knows barren women who'd give anything they could for a chance to have a healthy baby. I birthed most o' the babies on the plantation, I did, even the babies at the big house. Ain't nobody in these parts better at birthin' babies than Becca Weaver." She pointed a chubby finger at Jenny and wagged it. "An' I says no dancin'!"

Jenny chuckled. "We'll see. Tell me something, Becca. Just how are we to accomplish this great vanishing? Won't the neighbors suspect something?"

"Law, no! Yo' aunt's already gone to the dressmaker to order some new clothes for a 'journey.' Out West, on a train! In fact, you gonna have a fitting sometime in the next few days."

Now Jenny's eyes got big. "You mean they would go that far to deceive?"

"Even further. Yo' mama's asked that ol' Miz Cathcart from across the street—the one with the broom handle up her nose—to come help her plan your itin ... iter ... "

"Itinerary. That is unbelievable!"

"Pretty smart, I'd say. You still got a little time before you starts showin', so why not get it planned out?"

Jenny shook her head. "This is all so silly. Pretending I'm going on holiday, when I'll be right here in this house! Why can't I just have my baby and be proud of it?"

"Things ain't done that way, honey. Least ways not in the white fo'ks world."

"I really can't see how this solves anything. What happens after my baby is born? After I return from my fictitious journey? What then? Will my baby be hidden away in the attic until it is grown, for heaven's sake?"

Becca looked down at the floor.

"Well, Becca? How do they plan to take care of that little problem? How do we explain the sudden appearance of a baby? Did I find it in a basket, abandoned on a train out West? Better yet, how do we explain it in London?"

Becca pushed herself out of the chair and sat beside Jenny on the bed. "Honey chile," she said, taking Jenny's hand. "This ain't easy for me to say, an' I prob'ly shouldn' be the one sayin' it, but ... the baby won't be goin' back to London with you."

Jenny bolted upright. "What do you mean?"

"I means, no one's ever goin' to know you had a baby."

"You're going to kill my baby?" She jerked her hand away.

"No! Oh, darlin' no! Becca would never do no such a thing!"

"Just what would you do?"

"I've got my 'structions."

"What instructions? Becca, get on with it!"

Becca sighed, bracing herself, and looked straight at Jenny. "I'm to take the baby to a wet nurse, an' when it's weaned, I'm to give it to a good family. Believe me, chile, yo' baby's goin' to a family who'll love it jes' like you would. I've already picked 'em out, a nice white couple who can never have no chillun o' their own, one o' those barren women I mentioned afore. They don' have much money, but they got lots o' love in their hearts. They'll take good care o' yo' baby."

~~~

For the next few days, Jenny endured fittings for dresses she would never wear and ridiculous conversations with Mrs. Cathcart about places she would never see. Millicent had even produced last year's copies of *The Strand*, containing Conan Doyle's serial, "Adventures of Sherlock Holmes," sure that Jenny would enjoy reading it on her "journey." Either her mother's mind was slipping, or she fancied herself the greatest actress who ever lived.

During this time, Young Moses was busy in the attic. Under Millicent's direction, he put new frames around the sections of the big Palladian window and covered the whole thing with heavy, brocade draperies. He polished the walls and the floor and laid an enormous area rug in the center. Next, and with great difficulty, he carried a chest of drawers, a table, two straight chairs, a small sofa, several kerosene lamps, and an overstuffed chair from the trunk room.

When Jenny saw it all, she nearly had a fit.

"Aunt Violet!" she screamed.

Violet came running up the attic stairs. "What is it, Jenny? What's wrong?"

"*This* is what's wrong!" She indicated her transformed dance studio with a grand sweep of the arms. "What, exactly, is it supposed to *be*?"

Violet looked around, then burst into gales of laughter. "I believe it is supposed to be your new sitting room."

"I don't need a place to *sit*, for heaven's sake! I need a place to *dance*!" But Violet's laughter was infectious. Jenny giggled and then she, too, laughed. "It's hideous, isn't it? Like an assembly of cast-offs."

"I am sure that is exactly what it is," Violet replied, catching her breath. "Most of it came from the trunk room, but I remember seeing that purple sofa and the extra lamps in the unused bedroom at the rear of the house."

"I guess if we roll up the rug and move the table away from the ballet bar, there will be enough room to exercise at least. I only wish he hadn't polished the floor!"

"Now, Jenny, you are going to have to forget about dancing for the time being."

"Oh, posh! Exercise never hurt anybody. I don't plan to do leaps or *frappés.*

"I should hope not. Let's sit a moment, dear."

"On that purple thing?"

"On the purple thing." Violet smiled. "Now, then, we shall be spending the next several months together on these upper floors, and—"

"Oh, Aunt Violet, I hate it that you're confined with me. That is so cruel!"

"No, no, dear. Don't give it another thought. I would much rather be up here with you than floating around downstairs with your mother and her friends. I never was much of a social butterfly. What I started to say was, let's fill our time with meaningful pursuits. Let's do a lot of reading and studying and discussing, particularly of current events. I shall choose books from the library downstairs—some of the classics, of course, but also some for pure enjoyment. I know you have not read Edward Bellamy's fantasy, *Looking Backward, 2000-1887.*"

"Oooh!" Jenny squealed. "Could we? I cannot imagine life in the year 2000!"

"Well, we shall see how Mr. Bellamy imagines it." Then Violet's eyes twinkled and she said, "The Epworth League is having a literary meeting next month. I wish we could be there to hear the discussion. It would be great fun."

"Fun? A boring evening, you mean."

"Not so," Violet said. "The topic will be, *Our English Ancestors Were Heathen.*"

Jenny whooped with laughter.

"That truly is the topic," Violet said, joining the gaiety. "I don't think they would appreciate our presence!" Then she became serious again. "Also, we shall have Becca bring us a copy of that new magazine, *Vogue*—we can keep up with fashion—and a copy of *The Times* each week."

"A newspaper? You know what Father thinks of ladies reading

newspapers."

"I know. Very unsuitable. But I do not agree. This is a good time to study American politics. It is an election year, and, for the first time, they are introducing the Populist Party to challenge Republicans and Democrats."

"I don't understand any of that," Jenny said dismissively.

"But you should. You are a bright young woman, and we are going to keep your mind stimulated. You were meant for much more than tea parties and a bit of needlework."

"Oh, Aunt Violet, I had such dreams. I was going to study with Catherine Kingsley while we were here, and then meet Katti Lanner and become a famous dancer. None of that will happen now!"

"Don't give up your dreams, Jenny. Don't *ever* give up your dreams! That is why I want you to exercise your mind as well as your body. You can do anything you put your mind to! Having a baby only takes nine months. That's a very little bit of a lifetime."

"I'm not sure I want to give my baby away."

"I can sympathize with your feelings, dear, but I do believe, at your age, it is best. It's best for you; and, think of your baby—it is best for a baby to be reared by two parents, free of stigma."

Though it hurt terribly, Jenny knew in her heart that Violet was right. Her baby could never grow up in London, the child of an unmarried … child.

Chapter 14

At least Jenny's baby would grow up, Andrea thought, with a touch of bitterness. She pulled her cramped leg out from under her and rose from the swing. Her foot was asleep, so she stomped it as she walked through the house to the kitchen. It was already lunchtime and she still had the third diary to read.

She pulled some potato salad from the refrigerator and sliced a big tomato that Mr. Pinckney had grown next door, then took the food to the picnic table in her backyard. A big pecan tree cast lacy shadows over her lunch.

"I don't mind sharing my tomatoes at all," Mr. Pinckney had said, "because your tree drops pecans in my yard every year!" He was a funny neighbor, but Andrea liked him.

She sat facing the carriage house. In the years since Becca Weaver lived above the carriages, the building had been converted to apartments, upstairs and down. It was now separated from Alex's and Andrea's yard by the picket fence that ran all around, but it remained part of their property and they collected the rent. She could imagine Becca moving around upstairs and Young Moses working below with his tools. *Dear God, it is all so real!* Would she ever be able to shake loose of the Alcott family and their troubles? Or would they haunt her for the rest of her life?

Andrea had begun having uncomfortable dreams—not

nightmares, just dreams she couldn't remember, dreams that left her with an empty feeling. Now, as she studied the carriage house, she had that feeling again. There was an empty space within her that needed to be filled.

She swallowed the last bite of her lunch, then stood, tossing her paper plate and plastic fork into the trash can. She started walking up the street, looking at the lovely old houses and the yards that were, unlike hers, neatly raked and trimmed—unnecessarily turning fall into spring, she thought. Within a few blocks she found herself at the "Big Oak," a 320-year-old tree that now was protected by the city. It was a beautiful monster, draping across all four corners of an intersection, its heavy branches resting on metal stanchions. As always, there were a few tourists beneath it, snapping photos.

Andrea had been there before, but this time she was acutely aware of the fact that Jenny Alcott had been there, too. The tree, then at 200-plus years, would already have become huge. She touched its trunk, picturing Jenny seated on one of the low-slung limbs—before her pregnancy, of course. Andrea still didn't know what had happened after that.

On she went, circling the block, trying to work the stiffness out of her muscles, particularly her neck and upper back. She passed the post office, then glanced across the street, stopping suddenly. There was First United Methodist Church, the one that Jenny had referred to as the Methodist Episcopal Church, the one where she had prayed to God for help, while her mother was meeting "all the right people." Andrea had never been inside (she was a "Babdis") and, now that she knew the Alcotts had attended there, she wanted to see it for herself.

Quickly, she crossed the street, climbed the wide stone stairs, and opened the huge door. Up one more flight of stairs and she was in the enormous sanctuary. The sight stunned her. It was of another world, another era—Jenny's era—and it nearly took her breath away! This was a sanctuary of fully restored Victorian splendor. There were wooden arches and pillars, needlework kneeling cushions, and replicas of gaslight chandeliers.

Andrea walked slowly down the aisle, running her hands over the carvings at the ends of the old wooden pews. She smiled as she thought of the spittoons Jenny had called "nasty." There were none here now.

Where did Jenny and her family sit? In the back? The front? The middle? Did Jenny return here after the baby was born? Did she ever marry? At this altar, perhaps? Andrea knelt briefly, her elbows on the altar, her head resting in her hands. *I just can't forget about the Alcotts*, she thought.

After a few moments of quiet, she rose and left. *Maybe it's not time to forget. Maybe I have to see it all the way through, for my own peace of mind.*

~~~

Back at the house, she picked up the last diary and settled into the recliner in the den. This book was crammed with papers of all sorts—notes, recipes, letters, even faded photos and a few tintypes. The first one, taken on the front steps of the house, had to be of Jenny. She was looking directly into the camera and smiling, a very un-Victorian thing to do! Andrea smiled back. What a lovely girl! Her dark hair was piled high on her head, but wispy strands popped out everywhere. Her dress was high-necked and long-sleeved, and a deep, bouncy ruffle formed the hem. Imp that she was, she had pushed one pointy shoe forward so it could be seen. Most arresting, though, were her laughing eyes—dark and deep-set. They pierced clear to the core of Andrea's soul.

"I am glad," Andrea said aloud, "that you had something to be happy about, at least on that one day."

As she began to read, Andrea found that Jenny had neglected her diaries for many weeks; and, when she did write, it was in "snippets," she said, because she was bored. There was not much to write about, despite Violet's attempts to keep her mind stimulated.

~~~

"Isn't there something we can do, Aunt Violet?" Jenny pleaded. "I need an adventure, or I shall go positively mad!"

"An adventure, hmm? To tell the truth, so do I. Let me think ...."

"Why don't we sneak out of here one day and go somewhere?" Jenny suggested. "Anywhere!"

"I know what you mean. Fresh air would be a treat." Suddenly Violet's face lit up like a child's. "What about day after tomorrow?"

"Day after tomorrow?"

"Yes. Your parents will be at the Mitchell House Hotel all day working to raise funds for the new railroad. We could go out then."

"Oooh," Jenny squealed. "But how will we keep from being recognized?"

"Disguises, of course." Violet's voice took on a youthful lilt. "Becca could have Young Moses bring us some clothes."

"Do you think she would help?"

"I would not put her in that position. I shall tell her we need some old clothes and let her think what she will."

They had great fun dressing up in layers of worn, drab clothing. Becca had even thrown some tattered bonnets in with the lot. Then Violet sent Young Moses to the backyard for a little pail of dirt.

"Ma'am ... you wants *dirt?*" he asked.

"Yes, Young Moses, and please hurry. We need it right away."

"You want some flower seeds 'n pots?"

"No, just dirt."

"Upstairs, here?"

Jenny glared at him until he backed out of the room.

"Yes'm," he said. "I'll bring a pail o' dirt upstairs right away." As he walked away, he mumbled, as he had done so often, "Sho' don' un'erstand white fo'ks!"

A short time later they met Becca on the landing, and Becca nearly tumbled backwards down the stairs.

"Law! Miz Violet, you scared me half to death! An' is that Miz Jenny? Why you dressed up in those ol' clothes? I thought you was gonna use 'em fo' patchwork. Uh-oh ... you plannin' to sneak outta here?"

Jenny giggled. "How do we look?"

"You looks like a sho'nuf mess an' that's the truth! What's that on yo' face, chile?"

"Dirt. It's all over me," Jenny said proudly, holding out her skirts.

"I can see that. It's gonna be all over the rug, too. I don' know 'bout this, Miz Violet. Seems to me you two is askin' fo' a heap o' trouble."

"It will be worth it, Becca," Violet answered, pushing past her. "We haven't breathed the outside air for months. Oh, I feel young again! Come along, Jenny!"

Becca leaned over the rail. "You take a bit o' advice from ol' Becca. You keep yo' mouths shut, 'cause soon as someone hears the funny way you talk, they sho'nuf gonna know who you is!"

Jenny laughed as they headed for the back door. "Maybe I ought to take some flowers along. I truly look like a London flower girl— a fat one!"

"Oh, hush! They don't have flower girls here. Pull that bonnet around your face."

What a wonderful day they had! They went down Broad Street, taking their good time. Sheriff Doss was in front of the courthouse, checking on the yardwork. He liked to keep it in "neat trim," as he had told Jenny's father. But they didn't dare speak to him, lest they be discovered.

They stood for a long time in front of the milliner's window, inspecting the latest creations—colors, materials, ribbons, feathers. What fun! Then they went into the bookseller's and watched him use his new telephone. He talked rather loudly into the mouthpiece, so they could hear him just fine, but it was impossible to hear anyone on the other end. They stood close as they dared until he glared at them, then left quickly.

"Amazing!" Jenny said, once they were outside. "How do you suppose it works? I want one!"

"Whomever would you talk with?"

"Evelyn, of course."

"Evelyn! All the way to England? Don't be silly."

"I have an idea," Jenny said suddenly. "Let's go down to the Piney Woods Hotel and ride the elevator."

Violet grinned and mimicked the hotel slogan: "Where North and South Meet and Mingle. And which are we?"

"Oh, South, I should think. We hardly look like Yankees today."

"Jenny, how vulgar!"

"Well, that is what they call Northerners."

So they went to the Piney Woods—a rambling, turreted, frame structure made entirely of yellow pine inside and out—and rode the elevator. Up and down they went, several times. Only the elevator operator's practiced dignity kept him from reprimanding them. For all he knew, they could be guests, albeit strange ones. He kept his eyes straight ahead.

"What are you thinking?" Jenny whispered, watching Violet's smiling face.

"I am thinking that if children have this much fun, then I was never a child."

They rode until a guest began taking a curious interest. "She is a Yankee," Jenny said as they left. Violet poked her in the ribs.

Next, they went across the street to the opera house and read the placards out front.

"Hettie Bernard Chase will be here on Wednesday the fourteenth of December," read Violet aloud.

"Who is she?" Jenny asked, as she tried to open the door. All she wanted was to look inside.

"I have no idea," Violet answered.

Just then the door was jerked open from the inside, and stage manager Spence sent them packing.

"Here now. Off with you!" he said. "Can't have your kind around here."

They hurried back down Broad Street in a fit of giggles. "Just what 'kind' are we, Aunt Violet?"

"The dirty kind. That is obvious. Why don't we go to Mr. Moller's photography shop? Are we not worthy of a photograph?"

"Oh, Aunt Violet," Jenny said, laughing, "you are the most

wonderful person I have ever known! You make me feel happy when I have no reason nor right to be. I do love you so!"

"I love you, too, dear. Maybe too much. Whenever I am torn between doing what is right and what is frivolous where you are concerned, I always seem to choose the frivolous."

"Is that so bad?"

"I don't really know. I cannot help feeling responsible for your problem."

"You are not in the least responsible. I acted entirely on my own and you know that."

"But I encouraged you to see Tyler."

"I did not need much encouragement, Aunt Violet. I was completely taken with him from the very beginning."

"I suppose so. It's just that I … I was seeing myself, the young Violet Alcott, in you … and I wanted so much for you to find the romance, the love, that I was never able to have. What I truly regret is my naïve judgment of Tyler. I had no idea he was a rogue!"

"You were taken in, too. Don't blame yourself. He was a very good actor. He was so good, in fact, that I still find myself wondering if there could be some mistake, if Evelyn only imagined what she saw …. "

"Evelyn is not one to imagine things," Violet said.

Jenny sighed. "I know. What I do not know, though, is how I would react if I were to see him again. I really did love him, and love is not all that easy to quell, even if Tyler is a scoundrel."

"Are you sure you don't want to tell him about the baby, Jenny? He does have a right to know."

"Never! He will never know about this baby. It is mine!" She patted her large tummy. "Little girl or little boy," she said, "you have had quite a day, dressed in rags and covered with dirt!"

As they rounded the corner toward home, Jenny said, "I am sorry this day is over. It has been marvelous fun! Thank you again, Aunt Violet."

They were laughing like children as they started to unlatch the back gate, but Millicent suddenly appeared at the back door. Startled, they could only stare—Jenny trembled a little—but it was soon obvious that Millicent did not recognize them. She gave them a very strange look and called out, "Is there something I can help you with?" Jenny pulled her bonnet further down on her face and turned away. Violet shook her head, raised her dirty hands high in the air and bowed deeply, as if she were mentally afflicted. Millicent stepped back into the doorway and the two ragamuffins took the opportunity to move on down the street. As they reached the corner, they heard her call out again, "Young Moses! Come wash this gate at once! I'm late for an appointment with the bootist."

Jenny peeked around to see her mother hurrying in the opposite direction, toward Broad Street. "She wasn't supposed to be here!" she whispered, much too loudly.

"Shh! She must have forgotten to leave fabric swatches at the bootist's on her way to the hotel. Her reticule is stuffed to overflowing. Wait a few moments. As soon as she is out of sight, we shall go back."

Just then a wagon and two ponies out of control came down Dawson Street, kicking the dust up into big clouds. When they had passed, Jenny and Violet looked even worse than before. The incident appeared in the weekly *Thomasville Times*, but of course (and thankfully!) the reporter had no knowledge of London ladies being nearby.

When Millicent finally disappeared around the opposite corner, Jenny and Violet returned to the back gate and slipped into the house.

"Law! Don' you never give me no mo' trouble like you did this day!" Becca cried as soon as they were inside. "When I sees you comin' in the back gate an' Miz Millicent a' goin' out, I prayed the good Lord to take me home right that minute so I wouldn' have to suffer any more on this earth, but he didn', he worked it out hisself. Now, Miz Violet, I got no right talkin' to you this way, but you give me a *fright*, yes you did! Now what you ladies, who don' look like ladies a'tall, what you got to say fo' yo'selfs?"

Violet and Jenny had been staring at her. Violet suddenly burst out laughing and Jenny tore off her grimy bonnet and tossed it into the air. "It was wonderful!" she shrieked.

"Absolutely splendid!" Violet agreed.

"Hmmph—'splendid'!" Becca mocked. But she could keep up the pretense no longer. She broke into a wide grin, then began to laugh, slowly at first, then more intensely, until her whole body shook. "You two's a real mess!" she said, finally. "Go on, now, git those rags off an' I'll have Young Moses burn 'em."

It had been a most *marvelous* adventure!

Chapter 15

Jenny's adventure made Andrea laugh, and it recalled to mind her own adventure—the time she spent with "worldly" Aunt Mary in Birmingham. She had stayed for a year, and, until the birth of her baby, the entire time was an adventure. After that, well, things changed. But Aunt Mary Cooper was always a delight—a lot like Violet Alcott—and she never made Andrea feel bad or guilty or ashamed.

"What's done is done," she had said. "We don't worry about what happened or why. Our only concern is, 'What do we do next?' I say we do everything possible to ensure a happy mother and a healthy baby. And there'll be no hiding in this house. You're my niece and you're having a baby, and I can't wait to shop for tiny little clothes and bibs and rattles!" She gave Andrea a big hug. "I'm glad you're here."

"You don't … you're not worried about what people, well … what they'll think?"

Mary smiled. "My friends don't care, and the others don't matter."

Andrea's eyes misted at the memory. Alex had spoken similar words not long ago and she had been critical of him. It was the way she'd been brought up. Even now, after so many years, openness was extremely difficult to achieve.

"Here, now," Aunt Mary had said so long ago. "There's no need for tears. We've got a lot to do. We're going to make the extra bedroom into a nursery."

"Aunt Mary—"

"Please call me Mary," she said. "I'm not but twelve years older than you, and I'd much rather be treated like a big sister."

Andrea nodded, gratefully. She still couldn't believe her mother had sent her to this pretty little cottage and to this wonderful person. It was entirely out of character for Doris.

"Mary," she said. "What about after the baby is born? What then? Can you help me find work and a place of my own to live? Mother won't have me back home with the baby."

"You 'made your bed and you can sleep in it.' I know. She told me. Like I said before—we'll look forward, not back. And yes, I'll help you find work, maybe even in the same office I'm in. We have a large secretarial pool and there's always a need for smart young people. As for where you'll live, I'd be perfectly happy to keep you and the baby here with me." Andrea started to protest, but Mary continued, "I'd enjoy the company, and you could pay rent, if that would make you feel better."

The arrangement was more than satisfactory; and, with her worries set aside, Andrea was able to concentrate on a healthy diet and exercise, to help weed the garden, decorate the nursery, shop for baby clothes, and, quite frankly, to enjoy her pregnancy. *Imagine writing* that *home to Mother*, she thought: *I'm enjoying my pregnancy.* Doris Cooper would faint dead away. Pregnancy was a dirty word, almost as bad as sex.

Doris did write once a month. She sent news from home, which didn't amount to much, and she quoted scripture that she felt would be helpful. Andrea often thought her mother should have been a preacher, except that women did not do such things in those days, at least not in the circles Doris traveled. Women didn't even teach Sunday School as long as there was a capable man available. Inside Doris' letters there was always a small check for Mary, which Doris said was her Christian duty to provide, along with a word of caution to Andrea not to emulate Mary's "ways." She never mentioned the

approaching birth, and she never signed her letters, "Love, Mom."
Simply, "Mother."

"What's the matter?" Mary asked one day after Andrea had read
one of Doris' letters.

"I feel empty. I always feel empty after reading my mother's
letters, and I can't really explain it. My childhood was reasonably
happy."

"Your parents were very strict, Andrea."

"True, but they were good to me. Mom was a wonderful cook,
and she shared her secret recipes with me and taught me how to
make them. She sewed my bedspread herself, and curtains—even
let me choose the material."

"You were lonely, though. I remember hearing you say more than
once that you wished you had a brother or sister."

"That was after my best friend, Beth, moved away. There were
other neighbor children but no one I could really talk with, confide
in." Andrea smiled. "I started telling my private thoughts to my stuffed
animals."

These memories and others like them washed over Andrea with
every letter that arrived at Mary's house. She was sorry that she had
disappointed her mother, but even more sorry that Doris had lacked
warmth, because, underneath it all, she had loved her mother and
missed her very much.

~~~

Jenny's baby was born on New Year's Day, 1893. Becca delivered
a girl, the most beautiful, dainty little girl Jenny had ever seen. She
had tiny tufts of dark hair, dark eyes, and skin the color of fresh
cream, and Jenny named her Evelette.

"For my two favorite people, of course—Evelyn and Violet," she
said.

Violet sat there in the bedside chair, but she did not respond. She
couldn't. And Jenny knew why—because the baby would soon be
taken away. She could see Violet's lip trembling, but she was sure

there was nothing to worry about. How could her parents possibly give this beautiful baby away, especially now that they'd seen her? True, her father had only stood in the doorway, and her mother had merely peeked in. Still ….

She held Evelette in her arms, letting the tiny fingers curl around her own. "Look at her nails, hardly bigger than needles' eyes!" she said to Violet.

She was so enthralled with Evelette, that she stayed awake all that first night. She recited rhymes and hummed little tunes and watched every tiny movement with her heart full of more love than she had ever known. Nothing in her short life could ever compare to this! Not even what she had felt for Tyler Fleming. Though her pride still suffered, she could now look back on that time, and on him, merely as an episode. She had finally accepted the fact that he was a rogue and a scoundrel and that she had been a gullible child.

She played with Evelette for several more days—in bed, of course, on Becca's orders. But then one day Becca came into the room carrying a large basket lined with a soft, white blanket.

Jenny's face turned ashen. "No," she whispered, appalled by the realization of what was about to happen. "Becca, you cannot do this. Please don't do this!" She clutched her baby tightly to her body.

Becca sat down beside her on the bed, twisting her apron in her hands. "Honey chile, if there'd been any way a'tall, the baby would've been taken soon as it been borned. But the weather's been so bad, God knows we couldn' take that babe out in it fo' a long ride in a bumpy carriage! An' we couldn' bring the wet nurse here 'cause someone might've seen her. Miz Jenny, I don' want to do this any more'n you wants me to."

"Then don't!"

"Yo' papa says I have to. He's the boss, an' you're under age. I got no choice."

"Papaaaa!" Jenny screamed. Then she started to cry and so did the baby. Tiny Evelette could roar something fierce.

Barclay appeared at the bedroom door, looking a bit uncomfortable. "What is all this noise?"

"Evelette is my baby," Jenny sobbed, "and I want to keep her! Please don't take her away!"

"Now, Jenny, you know we cannot take a baby with us back to London."

"Then don't take *me* back—leave me here with her!"

"Be reasonable," he answered, shifting his weight. "Becca has found a good home for her. She'll be very happy."

"But *I* won't be happy. I love her and I want her. I cannot honestly believe you are serious about doing this."

"I am, indeed, serious, Jenny. There shall be no out-of-wedlock child in the Alcott home."

"But she's *my* child. She's *your* grandchild!"

Barclay's face turned purple. For a brief moment, he looked as if he would explode, but he recovered and quickly turned his attention to Becca. "Put the child in the basket. The sooner this is over, the better."

"Where's my mother? I want my mother!" Jenny cried.

"Your mother is lying on the parlor sofa in the midst of a spell, thanks to your screaming. She is not well enough to cope with your nonsense, Jenny, which is one more good reason to get this over with. Becca, do as you are told." He turned, clicking his heels like a wooden soldier, and marched down the stairs.

Becca heaved a great sigh, then slowly pried the baby from Jenny's shaking arms. She, too, had tears in her eyes. "I gives you my word, chile," she said. "This pretty little thing will grow up with a family what loves her an' will treat her right. That's a promise."

She put the baby in the basket and started for the door, tears rolling down her wide, brown cheeks. "Try to get some rest," she said, kindly.

But Jenny could not rest! Her body was burning with rage and helplessness. She rose up in bed and sobbed, her arms stretching toward her baby, "Evelette! Evelette ... I won't forget you. I won't!"

"This breaks my heart," Becca whispered, more to herself than to Jenny. "Jes' breaks my heart." And she took Evelette away.

~~~

Andrea's baby was born on April Fool's Day, and Andrea was the victim of the bitterest of April Fool's jokes—her son was born dead. He had strangled on the umbilical cord just before seeing the light of day. There was no help for it, because he was born in a taxicab on the way to the hospital.

It happened two weeks before the baby was due. Mary had left for work early, and Andrea hadn't wanted to disturb her at the office, so she called the taxi herself. But she had waited too long to call, then waited for the cab to arrive, then waited even longer as Birmingham's heavy rush-hour traffic slowed the cab to a crawl. Finally, when it wasn't possible to wait any longer, the frantic driver—who was terrified at the prospect of delivering a baby—stopped the cab, got outside and screamed for help.

Two women left their cars in the street and tried their best, but neither knew what they were doing, and everyone else just sat in their vehicles and blew their horns impatiently. A policeman arrived, but too late. The strangled baby was a breech birth, and Andrea was unconscious and losing blood. Finally, in the hospital emergency room she was a victim once again, this time of a hysterectomy to save her life.

When she awakened hours later, Mary was standing beside the bed, holding her hand, trying to smile. Andrea could see she'd been weeping.

"It's all right," Mary said. "It's all right. You're alive, and that's all that matters."

" … My baby?"

Mary shook her head. "He didn't make it."

Andrea swallowed hard and closed her eyes. "He? … I had a son?"

"Yes."

Tears stung her eyes. "What happened?"

So Mary explained, as best she could, all that had been relayed to her. "You almost died, Andrea," she added, "but I'm so thankful you didn't."

She leaned over and kissed Andrea's forehead, then pulled a chair up close to the bed. "I've arranged some time off so that I can be with you when you come home, just as we'd planned if the baby had lived. I'm going to take care of you. You mustn't worry about anything."

Andrea the teenager, however, was crying. She felt sick. "It was all my fault. I waited too long to call the cab. But I didn't know for sure. It didn't hurt. I thought … I thought labor pains were supposed to hurt, but they didn't, not at first. That's why I wasn't sure. I'm stupid!" she sniffed.

Mary handed her a tissue. "There was no way you could have predicted this. You've never had a baby before. For that matter, neither have I, so I probably wouldn't have been much help. You did the best you could, and you cannot second-guess yourself. Neither of us suspected that the baby would come early, especially not that early. There was no warning."

"But he would have lived!" Andrea cried. "If I hadn't been so stupid, my son would be alive!"

"Your intelligence has nothing to do with it. Andrea, you can't drench yourself in guilt over this. It was not your fault. Understand that. You have been made to suffer guilt all of your life over one thing and another, and I'll not let you carry any more of it. As soon as you're able, you are coming home with me, and we're going to put your life back together. You're an adult, Andrea. A fine human being … much too fine to waste."

When Andrea arrived at Mary's cottage, she expected that the nursery would be dismantled and the baby gifts put out of sight, but they weren't. Mary had left everything exactly as it was, so they could do it together. It took several days, and they cried a lot. The whole process was emotionally painful, especially taking the lovely new baby clothes to Goodwill; but when it was over, it was really over.

"Mary, you're wonderful," Andrea said. "I couldn't have survived any of this without you. In the first place, I'd have been pregnant and on the streets."

"Oh, I doubt that. Your mother's a hard one, but if it came right down to it, she'd take care of you. She loves you, Andrea, she really does, in her own strange way. Doris wasn't always like she is now, you know."

"She wasn't?"

"No. It was marrying into the Cooper family that changed her. Your father was the best of the lot, but the others put the pressure on her. Doris Meade actually was a very sweet and loving person in the beginning, but over the years she got just like them—long-nosed, tight-lipped, and narrow-minded. I should know how they are, since I'm one of them! Or was. Well, I guess I still am a Cooper—I just don't *think* like they do."

"Did you grow up with guilt, too?"

"Oh, yes. It's their favorite weapon."

"But you didn't do what I did."

"I didn't do, period. That was the problem," Mary said. "I didn't cook, didn't sew, didn't get ecstatic over polishing the kitchen floor, and I wasn't interested in getting married young. I wanted to work and earn my own living. Not normal, they said. The Cooper family believes that life should be lived according to a pattern. You know that, Andrea. It's a Divine pattern, so they say—husband earns the living, wife stays home. An independent female doesn't fit into it, though that's changing now, thank goodness! Mysteriously, education is becoming part of the pattern. An unmarried mother, however, is still a problem that's difficult to deal with. There's no rationale to explain it away."

"But why turn against us? That's not right either."

"They don't actually turn against us. It's more a matter of not knowing what to *do* with us. In my case, they allowed me to find my own way while they sat back and watched, and waited for me to fail. When I didn't fail and didn't go running home to the fold, they grudgingly acknowledged me as a maverick."

"Mother calls you 'worldly,'" Andrea said with a smile.

Mary laughed. "I know. But I also know that if I ever needed anything, Doris would be the first to offer help."

Andrea sighed. "I wish I hadn't disappointed her so much."

"There you go again. Get rid of the guilt and look forward! Do something to make her proud."

Do something to make her proud. Andrea thought about that for several weeks. And when she had it all worked out in her mind, she called her mother. That's when they talked about college, about going to Georgia State.

Doris tried to sound tough, but Andrea could hear the break in her voice. "Come home, Andrea," she'd said.

~~~

Andrea looked up from the diary, her emotions nearly as tattered as Jenny's. *Why can't I just read it,* she thought, *and stop thinking about myself? Why do I keep stomping over old ground, digging up old bones? What's the purpose, Jenny? Why are you putting me through this?* She didn't like what it was doing to her, but she could no more quit reading the diaries than stop breathing. She had to know … what happened to Jenny Alcott? What happened to Evelette? And what would all of it mean to Andrea Ferris now, in the twenty-first century?

Shaking off her feelings, she turned to the back of the diary and leafed through the loose papers. There were some photographs— one of Becca Weaver and Young Moses standing at the back gate, broad white grins on their dark faces; and one of a lovely, blond young woman in a fashionable traveling gown and fur muff, which seemed out of place in South Georgia. Andrea turned that one over, but there was no identification. She looked at the photo again, definitely taken in front of the Alcott's carriage house.

She set it aside and lifted the next, a sepia-tinted likeness of Millicent and Barclay Alcott. Millicent looked a bit dotty, Andrea thought, and Barclay had the proverbial broom handle up his nose. She tucked that one back into the book. Next was a lovely photo with "Violet" written across the bottom, and this one surprised Andrea. She'd pictured Violet as looking much older, but she was young and beautiful. Of course, by nineteenth-century standards, she supposed a woman of thirty might have been considered past her prime.

There were some letters from Evelyn, which she would read later, after she'd finished the diary, and there was a small envelope marked "Evelette." Andrea opened it very carefully. Inside was a tiny tuft of fine, dark hair ... all Jenny had been left with. Andrea nearly wept. She didn't have a sprig of her own son's hair. All she had were memories, and they were not good.

The next loose paper cheered her up considerably. It was a recipe: "Becca's Apple Pie." She pushed herself up out of the chair and took the recipe to the kitchen. There wasn't time now, but tomorrow afternoon—Sunday—she would bake it for Alex. He loved apple pie, and she'd never been very good at it. Sure, she could do a great apple strudel and a honey-baked apple that would bring him to his knees, but she'd never really mastered an old-fashioned pie. Becca's recipe looked like fun, especially converting such listings as "six half-eggshells of water!"

She glanced at the clock. It was a little past three, and the weather was good—sunshine and cool breezes. She'd enjoyed the swing the day before, so she filled a tall glass with iced tea and took the diary to the front porch.

It wouldn't be long now. She'd soon know what had become of Jenny Alcott. ... Maybe then she'd know what would become of Andrea Ferris.

Chapter 16

"But we cannot simply leave her here, Barclay!" Millicent wailed.

"We bloody well can!"

"Your language, Barclay, please."

"All right then, we *jolly* well can! You and I both know there'd be the devil to pay if we took her back to London now in the condition she's in. Sometimes I think the wretched girl stays sick on purpose."

"Now, Barclay, she has had a time of it. Becca says she needs complete bed rest for at least another month."

"Well, we cannot stay here another month. We have been here nearly a year already. If I don't take care of business in London now, there may not be any business left to take care of!"

"Barclay, that is not true. You know very well that your appointed officers are doing an excellent job of managing your assets. Now please calm down before you have a spell."

"If you ask me," he continued with slightly less volume, "Becca and Jenny are in cahoots."

" ... Ca-hoots?"

"An American word. Means conspiracy."

"Oh, Barclay, that is ridiculous."

"Admit it, Millicent. Jenny was perfectly fine until we took the baby away. I think she's trying to punish us and Becca is helping her."

Jenny was listening to their conversation through her open bedroom door. Actually, what her father had just said was true. She did not want to go back to London. She did not want to chance running into Tyler Fleming, and she did not want to make excuses to Evelyn and all the other girls who knew he had left her for someone else—Anne Whitehall, of all people!

When she had read about it in Evelyn's letter, she had been surprised as well as hurt. Anne Whitehall did not have any looks or grace to speak of—Evelyn was right when she compared her to a potato. But her family certainly had plenty of money; and, as Jenny had time to think about it, there was one more thing Anne Whitehall had plenty of. One thing that would matter a great deal to someone like Tyler Fleming. Breasts. Huge ones!

No, Jenny did not want to go back to London. She could not face all that nonsense, all that orderly, pretentious sophistication. To look at Anne Whitehall and pretend she didn't notice those huge breasts and was not thinking about who had been pawing them—indeed!

Jenny had grown to love the carefree life she'd been living in South Georgia, so different from anything she had known in childhood. Even her pregnancy, hidden away in the upper floors of the house, had been easy and pleasant. Violet had made it fun, and Becca had filled it with love. Jenny had done very well without those fussy little tea parties with scones and clotted cream. Instead, she had eaten generous portions of Becca's apple pie—her one craving during pregnancy—and learned with Violet about the dashing American West, so that the two of them could talk intelligently about their marvelous "journey!"

Barclay was right about Becca. Becca "sho' nuff" didn't want Jenny to go back to London. "Jes' like my own young'un, you are," she had said many times. "I don' think I can bear it when yo' daddy takes you away." Jenny couldn't bear it either. She loved being hugged close to Becca's ample figure, something else she had missed in childhood. Except for Violet's occasional squeeze, the Alcott family simply were not huggers. She knew Becca loved her and wanted to take care of her. But how could she bring it about? She certainly could not feign illness forever!

Jenny's turmoil had been nearly unbearable until Violet appeared in her room one night with The Great News: "Your father wants me to stay here with you for a few months, until you are well enough to travel. And he has offered to retain Becca and Young Moses to look after us." She punctuated her announcement with a wink.

Jenny had been overjoyed ... and since then she had become much, much more "ill."

Now, if her mother would just relent. She put her ear closer to the doorframe.

"I think you are wrong, Barclay," Millicent was saying. "However, since you are the man of the house, I have no choice but to abide by your decision."

Jenny sighed in relief. She wanted to run across the hall and throw her arms around her parents, but she did not dare run—that would give her away for sure. Though she was glad her father had won, she was surprised and pleased at the spirit her mother had shown. Confronting her husband, even that little bit, was something Millicent had learned since coming to the Colonies. And she hadn't had a "spell" in weeks!

Jenny tiptoed back to bed and propped herself up with several pillows. As soon as her parents were safely on their way to London, she would arrange a visit with Catherine Kingsley. If necessary, she would *beg* Miss Kingsley to accept her as a student. Jenny Alcott would become the most energetic and dedicated dancer the lady had ever known!

~~~

But once again her world turned upside-down.

On the voyage to England, Barclay Alcott's heart failed and he died. Millicent, upon disembarking, stepped in front of a fast-moving freight wagon and was crushed beneath its wheels. Onlookers reported that she had looked neither right nor left, that she seemed to have been in a "trance-like" state. That was certainly understandable, as Barclay had been her entire life, her means of identity, her reason for living.

~~~

Violet, as executrix, traveled to England to settle the estate, leaving Jenny behind with Becca. It was a good decision. Becca's arms were warm and loving. They were also protective, when Mrs. Cathcart and the neighborhood ladies came to pay their condolences.

"My li'l girl jes' ain't up to seein' no one right now, Miz Cathcart," she said. "I'm sho' you un'erstand."

"Well, yes, of course. Actually, we did not realize that she and Miss Violet had returned from their holiday out West, or we would have called sooner."

"Yes'm. They's been back a few weeks now, but was jes' so plum tuckered out they's stayed close to home. Now Miz Jenny's in mournin' besides. If you'd care to leave yo' cards, I'll tell Miz Jenny you called. I knows she'll 'preciate it."

"Oh. Well, yes, let's do that, ladies." They handed over their calling cards with appropriate kind words; and, after Mrs. Cathcart had adjusted her hat and her nose, they lifted their skirts and moved down the porch steps and out the front gate.

Jenny watched through the lace curtains and listened from her place on the parlor sofa. She was seventeen now, and she felt very old.

"Sit with me for a while, Becca," she said, tossing the calling cards into the bowl on the marble-top table. Becca eased her body into the overstuffed chair next to the sofa.

Jenny sighed. "Why can't I cry?" she asked.

"You've had a lot o' grownin' up to do in the last year, chile. It's been too much, too fast. You'll cry one o' these days. It jes' ain't yo' time yet."

"Do you think I did wrong, not going back to London with Violet?"

"No, I don't. Miz Violet didn' want you to go, and neither did I. She be back soon. You got a fine home here now an' a chance to start a brand new life. Miz Violet's letter said you can even buy this house, if you wants it. The owners, they ain't never comin' back."

"You know I want it. I want something else, too, Becca." The lift of her chin was no longer a childish tilt. It was the rock-hard look of a determined woman. "More than ever I want to be a great dancer ... and I mean to do it! I have decided I want to be spectacular, like Loie Fuller, but in my own way. I want audiences to love me. I am going to be *famous*, Becca!"

"I don' know who Miz Fuller is, but you sho' got the fixin's to be spectac'lar, chile."

"There is something else I want, too." She turned, looking pointedly into Becca's eyes. " ... And you are the only one who can give it to me."

"Anything, chile. Anything at all."

Jenny's chin shot up again. "I want Evelette back."

Becca's hands tightened on the arm of her chair, and she sat up a little straighter. "Now, Miz Jenny, you know that's the one thing I cain't give. You knows that."

"Yes you can! What difference does it make now? My parents are gone, and they are the only ones who cared a fig about what people think. Violet doesn't. And I certainly do not!"

Becca's face was pained. "That's not all there is to it, chile."

"What else is there?" Jenny was impatient.

"The other family, that's what. They've had that little girl fo' almos' six months now, and they love her like their own. They's no way I could take that baby from that nice mama now."

"You took her from me."

Becca's eyes watered. "That was a little different. Yo' daddy was in charge, 'cause you were underage. You had no say in it. I only did what I had to do." She sniffed, wiping her eyes on her apron. "It broke my heart, it did."

Jenny softened a little. "I know, Becca. I am sorry I upset you. But Evelette is *my* baby. I at least have a right to know where she is, so I can see her."

"I don' know 'bout that, chile." Becca shook her head. "I jes' don' know."

For the moment, Jenny took pity on Becca. Trying to show a little more gentleness, she changed the subject, "Why don't we have a tea party? Just you and me and Young Moses."

Becca's face lit up. "Now that's somethin' I do know about!" She pushed herself up out of the chair. "I'll go to the kitchen right now and bake some cookies."

"Not cookies, Becca. Pie. Apple pie."

"Apple pie?"

Jenny added, "With the cream that we iced last night."

Becca left the room chuckling.

And Jenny said to herself, *I am going to find her. I am going to find Evelette!*

~~~

Violet returned to Thomasville after four months in London. Barclay had left her and Jenny well provided for, and Violet was now Jenny's legal guardian. Barclay's business partner, Horace Morrison, had coveted the Alcott's London mansion for years, so Violet sold it to him, banking yet another considerable sum for Jenny's future. As for herself, she had little interest in money, except as it enabled her to purchase necessities. Jenny was her life ... and her life was in Thomasville.

Chapter 17

At this point, Jenny's interest in her diary became sporadic. The next few entries occurred six months later, but they were not personal—just notations about the weather and an occasional outing. She had scribbled, as if she felt obliged to make notes but was in too much of a hurry to make them worthwhile.

As Andrea leafed ahead, a full year had elapsed before Jenny was inclined to write again with any detail. Had she postponed her search for Evelette? Had she been too discouraged to write about it? Or had she thrown herself into dancing and lost interest in the rest of her life? From what Andrea knew about Jenny Alcott, only one of those options seemed possible—the obsession with dancing. Losing interest in Evelette? Never! Her child would always be there—cooing, gurgling, laughing, growing ... playing—playing with Jenny's mind ... and her heart. Andrea knew.

Maybe she would find the answers to all of her questions about Jenny within the last several pages of the diary. Maybe then she would know why Jenny had lured her to this house, to these diaries, at this particular time in her life. There was no doubt in her mind now—she had definitely been lured, but she still didn't know to what purpose. For her own peace of mind, she hoped fervently that she would find enough pieces to complete the mosaic that was Jenny Alcott. For the shape of her own future, she had to *know*.

She opened to Friday, August 10, 1894:

> *Dear Diary,*
> *Today I had the shock of my life! I was working in my*
> *attic studio, bending, stretching, twisting, and perspiring all*
> *over the place, when Becca came up the stairs with a calling*
> *card.*
> *It said,* Mrs. Angus Newton! ...

~~~

"Is this a joke, Becca?" Jenny asked.

"I don' think so. The lady has one o' them funny accents like you have."

"She's still here?"

"Said she'd sit on the porch swing 'til you came down to see her. Looked real cheerful, she did. Set that swing a-movin' right away. I s'posed she was a friend o' yours, Miz Jenny."

"I wouldn't exactly call Ada Gregory a friend. She was an acquaintance, Becca. I've told you about my friend Evelyn, haven't I?"

"Over and over."

"Well, Evelyn had a *marvelous* plan to fix Miss Gregory up with the man my parents wanted for me."

"Oh, my goodness!" Becca looked horrified. "Not the baby's—"

"No, no, no. Not Evelette's father. They did not like him, remember. Mr. Newton was a man I had refused to marry. An incredible snob with a chin long enough to reach all the way into a bucket of oats."

Becca chuckled. "Well, he sho' got hisself a pretty wife."

"Pretty? Ada's not pretty, at least she wasn't last time I saw her. Attractive, maybe, if it weren't for that mouse-colored hair."

"This lady's no mouse. She's a real beauty, an' her hair is the color o' corn silk."

Jenny was puzzled, but she laughed it off, saying, "I'll just have to meet her and clear up the mystery. Please bring up some water, Becca, then show the pretty lady into the parlor. I shall freshen up and be there shortly."

"Yes, ma'am. Oh, by the way," she called, as Jenny ran ahead of her down the attic stairs, "she's wearin' furs. *Furs* in a South Georgia summer! My goodness gracious—she'll have to push that swing mighty hard jes' to cool herself off!"

Jenny bathed as quickly as she could, then dressed in mint-green, a color that showed off her dark hair and reflected in her eyes. She couldn't imagine what Ada Gregory had done to herself to become so attractive, but whatever it was, Jenny Alcott would measure up. Why in the world was she here? What would make her leave the comfort of London society and Angus's money? Even if she were on holiday, a small town in Georgia was hardly the place of choice, unless one needed to "take the air" for bad lungs, as Millicent had pretended. That could be it—Ada had always sounded a bit wheezy.

A short while later Jenny went downstairs and stepped into the front parlor.

"Evelyn!" she shrieked. And both young women ran to each other's arms.

"Oh, Evelyn, it's been *forever* since I've seen you!"

"Two years, two months, and too long."

"Your calling card—it *was* a joke!" Jenny cried, pushing herself away so she could get a good look at her friend. "Mrs. Angus Newton, indeed!"

"No joke, Jenny, dear. I *am* Mrs. Angus Newton." She held out both hands, heavy with diamonds.

"What! But, Evelyn! Here, come sit down." She ushered Evelyn to the sofa. "I thought you were putting Ada Gregory in his path, though there was no need after my parents died. It was a game, your letters said, and everything was moving along fine."

"Everything *was* moving along fine. But he did not want Ada. He wanted me."

"And ... ?"

"And I thought about it and decided that a life of extreme luxury might suit me very well. I married him for his money, but actually, he turned out to be very sweet, and I like him very much. Guess I surprised you, didn't I?"

Jenny laughed. "Oh, Evelyn, you're a mess!"

"A what?" She looked at her clothes, and Jenny giggled some more.

"Not that. 'Mess' is an expression here. It means wonderfully crazy."

"Well, then I guess I am a mess!" Evelyn laughed.

"Now, for heaven's sake," said Jenny, "take off those furs before you die of heat stroke." Then she turned and yelled, "Becca, bring us some iced tea!"

"Goodness, Jenny, don't you have a bell?"

~~~

Evelyn had already dismissed the hansom. Her luggage was on the front porch awaiting Young Moses to carry it upstairs.

"So why isn't Angus with you?" Jenny asked. "How does it happen that he's allowed you to come all the way to the Colonies by yourself?"

"Allowed? Jenny, dear, I'm teaching Angus to be modern. He goes his way and I go mine. Right now he is in the Orient on business. But tell me about yourself. Tell me all that has happened since your last letter. Have you had the good fortune to find Evelette? How old would she be now? You were such a dear to name her for me, and for Violet, of course. Where is Violet, by the way?"

Evelyn still could go on and on, just like in the old days. "Violet is shopping," Jenny answered with a smile. "Evelette is eighteen months old, and I have had no luck with my search for her, though I shall admit I have not tried very hard—yet. There has not been much time, actually. Miss Kingsley is a tough taskmaster. She gives me two lessons a week and expects me to work myself to death in between!"

Evelyn's eyes twinkled. "How very good for you. Well, then,

150

while you work yourself to death, I shall take up the search for Evelette."

"What? Do you mean it? How long can you stay? More than just a few weeks, I hope!"

Evenly stood and announced triumphantly, "Four months! That is how long Angus will be in the Orient."

Jenny jumped up, whooping and squealing like a happy puppy, and tackled Evelyn with a hug that knocked them both onto the sofa, skirts flying.

Becca slipped in unseen, put the tray on the marble-top table, and left the room with a big grin on her face, mumbling, "Sho' is good to see Miz Jenny happy again!"

"What is Violet shopping for? Clothes? A new hat?" Evelyn asked, once they had collected themselves.

"Groceries."

"Groceries! Surely you have servants for that sort of thing."

"We have help, yes, but things are different here. Violet shops because she wants to."

"How extraordinary. You mean *everyone* does that?"

"No, not everyone. We don't worry about what everyone does."

Evelyn laughed. "Marvelous! You certainly have changed, Jenny. And your hair …." She gestured with one hand, holding her tea in the other. "You don't … well, *dress* it anymore, yet it looks lovely."

"It is clean, and it is out of my face," Jenny said, tightening the bow at the back of her neck. "A serious dancer cannot be bothered with hair."

"Or breasts, if I remember correctly!" Evelyn laughed again. "Oh, Jenny, it is good to be here with you. We have so much to talk about!"

For the next few days they talked, beginning with all the little things that were going on back home in London, changes that had taken place, friends that had married. Evelyn was full of news. They talked while strolling up and down Dawson Street, while swinging on the front porch swing, while devouring Becca's good food—quail soup, turnip greens, biscuits, honey-pecan balls and other specialties—and while Jenny danced in her attic studio.

"There is one more thing," Evelyn said on the fourth night. They were in the upstairs sitting room, both in their night clothes, ready for bed. "I have saved it for last, because I wanted to be sure you truly did not care a fig for Tyler Fleming. Do you still think it is best not to tell him about Evelette?"

"I will *never* tell that scoundrel!" Jenny was vehement.

Evelyn backed up, tilting her head. "I can see you are remarkably focused."

"Well? What is the news?"

"You're sure you don't care for Tyler?"

"I do not! Get on with it, for heaven's sake!"

"He's married."

Jenny's breath caught in her throat. It was true she did not care for him any longer. Still, he was her baby's father. She could not help but feel *something*. "Who ... who did he marry?" she asked, attempting brightness.

"Anne Whitehall, who else? He has been courting her almost since the moment you left. He is nothing but an idle rake now that he has a town house in Park Lane, a country home in Brighton, and a houseboat on the Thames. He was only after her money, Jenny. What else could it have been, except possibly those huge breasts!" She broke into giggles. "All men like those, even Angus, though I am sure he was disappointed in mine—little more than birds' eggs—once he saw me without all those stays that keep them pushed up and out!"

"Evelyn!"

Evelyn's eyes softened. "Jenny, are you sure you don't mind my telling you about Tyler?"

Did she mind? She had tried not to think about him at all during the past two years, but whenever she did, it hurt. Still, she was not sure what caused the hurt. Was it rejection—the trampling of her love, when she had given him her body, everything that was private and personal? Was it disillusionment? Breach of trust? Was it losing a father for her baby and her dreams of having a family? Did she really miss *him*? Or was it her pride that hurt the most? Yes, that was it. She had been snookered like a stupid fool, and that was a fact.

"Actually, Evelyn, I am glad he's married," she said. "I had already closed that door on my life … now I can lock it."

~~~

During the next weeks, Evelyn dabbled at searching for Evelette. She had no clear plan, only her own instincts, which were exceptionally good, but not good enough to break down walls of Southern loyalty.

"People are so clannish," she had said more than once. "They protect one another, even when they are not sure what it is they are protecting from!"

"You are an outsider," Jenny replied, "just like me. All either of us has to do is say 'good morning,' in our British way, which we cannot help, and they know that. It is not going to be easy."

Still, Evelyn persisted, often snaring Young Moses to take her in the carriage to farms in the country, looking for an adopted nearly-two-year-old with dark hair. Young Moses didn't mind, because she slipped him extra money. And it did not matter how often she asked him the same questions about what he knew, he would politely give her the same answer, "Don' know nothin', Ma'am."

"Of course he knows something, Jenny. His own mother took the baby away. He probably drove the carriage! Oh, dear. Do you suppose Becca gave Evelette to a Negro family? That would make it doubly difficult for *me* to find her."

"Not a possibility. If that were the case, the whole town would have been talking about it. No, Becca said she put Evelette with 'nice white folks' who would take her in as their very own and give her a good life. I believe she did just that. I also believe that the circle of people who know about Evelette is very small and very protective. They are not likely to talk."

"The family, whoever they are, have no doubt changed the child's name. If I mention 'Evelette' in my questions, I get nothing but wretched blank stares. You are probably the only person in the world who calls her that. I do wish we could get Becca to talk!" Evelyn stomped her foot.

"Becca refuses, at least for now. I do think she will tell me one day, perhaps when I am old and gray ... when it is too late." Jenny's eyes filled with tears, as they often did when she thought of her child.

Later that evening, she asked Becca a direct question. "Is her name still Evelette?"

Becca kept her eyes on the dough she was kneading, working it a little harder. "It's one o' her names," she said.

"Is it her second name?"

Becca shrugged.

"I know you won't lie to me, Becca. You simply won't answer if you think I am getting too close. So, it is her second name. Something like ... Elizabeth Evelette?"

Becca shrugged again. "Like that," she said.

Jenny relayed the information to Evelyn.

"Well! Next week I am going to visit several churches and talk with the vicars," Evelyn said. "Maybe the child was baptized. A name like Evelette is not easily forgotten, even when it is stuck in the middle. I should like to see one of the *vicars* lie to me!"

Jenny smiled. "For heaven's sake, don't call them vicars or maybe they *will* lie to you. They're preachers, Evelyn. Preachers."

"Very well," Evelyn sniffed. "I shall call on the preachers."

While Evelyn called on the preachers and everyone else she could discreetly visit, Jenny danced herself "nearly to death" preparing for her first important public performance. She had danced in several of Madame Dupré's recitals back in London, but they didn't count. She had been a child then.

Now, Miss Kingsley had engaged no less than the Opera House on Broad Street for the special recital, and tickets were sold out long before program details were finalized. Only the most accomplished students were invited to perform. A few professionals were coming from Atlanta to round out the program, and Miss Kingsley herself was going to dance! Everyone in town was excited—it was the favorite topic of conversation.

Jenny was wound up like a music-box doll, so excited she could hardly sleep at night. And having Evelyn with her to share the adventure was *marvelous*!

"I shall be dancing with gossamer wings attached to my wrists!" she said as she floated back and forth across the front porch.

Evelyn sat on the swing but held it still. "You mean like Loie Fuller?"

"Somewhat, but my dancing is much different. Miss Kingsley says I have a unique style, not quite like anyone she has ever seen— certainly not like anyone in America."

"But she approves?" Evelyn asked tentatively. Personally, from what she had seen in the attic studio, she thought Jenny's style rather unruly and a trifle indelicate.

"Of course she approves! She is not rigid like Madame Dupré." Jenny twirled, waving her arms with fluid motion. "She says I explore my inner feelings and *explode* them on the stage!"

Evelyn laughed, putting the swing in motion. "Jenny, I can hardly wait to see you explode!"

~~~

And explode she did, causing a flow of molten lava in the dancing world on her very first venture. Not only did she perform the solo she had prepared, but an encore as well! By the next day, newsboys were shouting her success from the street corners—"Local Miss Dances Her Way To Stardom!" Even ladies were discussing her flamboyant presentation behind their fans, including Mrs. Cathcart from across the street, who had not been in attendance because of a dreadful head cold.

"She said she wished she had not missed your performance," Evelyn related, "but I could not be sure how she meant it. She holds herself so strangely."

"Oh, Mrs. Cathcart's all right," Jenny replied. "The people here are genuinely lovely. They are just different from those we're used to. I am only sorry it took me so long to accept their friendship. Most of that was my own problem—I did not reach out, and they were reluctant to approach me. Think about it—if they seem so different to us, how in the world must we seem to them!"

"You need a new name."

"What? I thought we were discussing differences in people."

"That's what made me think of it. You need a new name for you new life. Something *different*."

The chains in Evelyn's thought processes were sometimes difficult to follow, but Jenny had long ago given up trying. "What are you talking about?" she asked.

"Something glamorous," Evelyn explained, gesturing grandly, "like ... Marguerita ... or Abigail. 'Jenny Alcott' simply does not sound like a *star*, and that is what you are going to be—a shining star!"

"It doesn't? I am?" Jenny breathed deeply, considering. Stardom was what she had always wanted, to be spectacular like Loie Fuller, and to be loved by everyone. Considering the accolades currently being heaped upon her, one might say she had begun her journey. Miss Kingsley had been most encouraging. She had suggested earlier, in fact, that Jenny remain in America permanently.

That thought had not quite taken hold in Jenny's mind until now. She'd been thinking that eventually she would have to return to London to build her reputation as a dancer, though she really did not want to go. Might it not be wise to build her reputation right here in the Colonies, where ordinary people seemed starved for truly good entertainment? Audiences would love her, as they did last night! Why should she go back to London and struggle, where the profession was already overcrowded? Why should she fight for space at the bottom of one of Katti Lanner's programs, when she could stay here and claim the top? Why, indeed?

"You are right, Evelyn," she said finally. "I am going to be a star. I truly am!"

"Of course you are. Now, what shall we call you?"

"Not Marguerita nor Abigail," Jenny replied, lured by Evelyn's enthusiasm. "And I do not care for Sophia, either. What about Millicent, my mother's name?"

"Too many memories. You do not need excess baggage, Jenny. Oh! What about Jennings? That would be a good surname, created right out of 'Jenny.' Something Jennings ... Caroline?"

"No, but I do have an idea. I read a name in a book once, when Violet and I were studying about the West, and I thought at the time that it was the most beautiful name I had ever heard, except—"

"Well? Except what?"

"Except that she was a saloon girl."

Evelyn giggled. "A saloon girl! What was her name?"

"Alissa."

"Alissssssa," Evelyn said, dragging out the s's. "Alissa Jennings. It's perfect!"

~~~

Andrea nearly spilled iced tea all over herself. Even *she* had heard of Alissa Jennings!

Jennings was the turn-of-the-century's "naughty but nice" girl. Her ballet technique was flawless, the height of cultural achievement, yet her choreography skirted the razor's edge of the risqué—just enough to cause blinks and gasps covered by discreet coughing and rapid fanning, but not quite enough to move her to the other side. To her advantage, she kept her personal life impeccable, unlike other popular entertainers of the time. Alissa Jennings was (almost) a lady in every sense!

Andrea took a deep breath, trying to remember. *There was a big event in the dance world on the twentieth anniversary of Jennings' death ... because she had established the climate for modern dance. A fundraiser for something ....* Yes! It was a few months before Andrea's twentieth birthday.

She had gone back to visit Aunt Mary Cooper during a break from her studies at Georgia State. Dance companies all over the country were staging spectacular productions at the same time on the same evening to raise money for something—she couldn't remember what. But she and Mary had attended the one in Birmingham, because Mary thought Andrea would enjoy it.

That would have been in 1981. That means Jenny died in 1961, Andrea thought. *That's the year I was born!* Jenny would have been in her late eighties.

Andrea took a long, slow drink of her iced tea, as a strange new thought took seed in her mind and began to grow. She hardly dared think it, but the idea was so tantalizing that she could not let it go: Since Jenny lived nearly ninety years, could Evelette, too, have had a long life? Could she still be alive? Andrea shook her head. Of course not. That would make her 108 years old. She paused. *But if Evelette did live well into old age ... even into her eighties ... she could have been alive as late as 1989 or 1990. Maybe the newspaper archives ... Maybe ....*

Chapter 18

Alex had plenty of time to think during the flight home. He was bearing gifts, and they had not been purchased by a secretary, nor had they been purchased out of guilt. He'd bought them before the Charlotte thing had happened. Hell, nothing had happened! Not that it couldn't have. He wasn't sure now how he'd have reacted if Andrea hadn't called, or even how he'd react under different circumstances. The body played funny tricks on the mind, even when the mind thought it was in control.

Since he'd met Andrea, he hadn't even considered another woman. He'd sure surprised himself this trip, though—first one way, then another. His initial reaction to Doug's idea of a fun night was *no way*. Then, for just a few seconds as Charlotte's hand moved up his thigh, he'd relaxed and thought *maybe*. Maybe it would have been fun, just one night. Andrea would never have known. *No, but I would have*, he admitted to himself. *And I'd have been damn sorry the next day*!

During the flight home he'd decided not to be a noble confessor. When he was young, his mother had said more than once, "Don't air your dirty laundry." So he wasn't going to air it. He was going to keep it in the hamper and clean it up himself.

Actually, he felt pretty good now. Business-wise, the trip had been well worth his time. He'd brushed up on family law, learned a few things about practicing in a small community, and done some networking for the future. He'd enjoyed himself, and frankly he was even grateful for Charlotte, because she had punctured his brain and made him think.

He could hardly wait to get home to Andrea. She'd been different since she'd found those diaries—more alive, not so moody and quiet. At least now she was interested in something. For the life of him, he couldn't figure why she was putting off her painting, her artwork. She had looked forward to moving, setting up a studio, and swirling wild colors all over big canvases. Why not get started, when that's what she'd wanted most of all? But she didn't talk about the "why not." She never liked to talk about herself. Of course if he were honest with himself, he had never encouraged her. With hindsight, that probably had been a mistake. Her pent-up feelings had finally scared the hell out of him.

He would encourage her now. When he got home, they would sit down and have a long talk about their dreams and fears, even about her growing-up years, if she could finally tell him. He'd make her understand that whatever was bothering her was important to him. *She'd got it wrong before. She'd thought I didn't care, but that was never the case.* He'd always cared, but he hadn't wanted to be intrusive. This time he would make it very clear. If she wanted to talk, he'd open the door wide and leave it open.

The first thing he wanted to do, though, was kiss her full on the mouth and take her upstairs to bed before they did anything else—no food, no wine, no talk, not even about those diaries!

~~~

Andrea picked up her iced tea and the remaining diary and went back into the house. Despite the warm autumn sun, she was shivering.

She didn't *plan* to go up the stairs and into the corner guest room, or to climb into Jenny's four-poster, or to pull the soft quilt over her legs. But that's what she did.

The curtain fluttered … and Andrea smiled and settled in.

Now she would finish reading the last diary. She had to learn all she could about the young Alissa Jennings, to have all the facts before … before what?

>*Dear Diary,*
>
>*Evelyn left last week, and we cried all over our new gowns. Honestly, having her here was most marvelous! She has given me courage to face the rest of my life. Not just courage, but determination. Before Evelyn came, my determination would flicker like a candle flame, because of what I really felt inside … scared and alone. I am still alone, but I am not afraid anymore. I will be a famous dancer. I will!*
>
>*At the moment, unfortunately, Becca is in bed with consumption. Poor dear. She is quite miserable ….*

Holy Moses came to visit. "Fo'ks gets consumption from tobacco-smoking, everyone knows that," he said. "But Becca, she ain't never smoked none. Mebby that fancy doctor's wrong. Mebby it ain't consumption."

"The doctor isn't wrong," said Violet, gently. "It is most definitely consumption, and she is very ill."

"Then why ain't he bleeding her? That's the only cure for it, 'cept for real fast horseback ridin', an' anyone can see she's not up to that!"

Mrs. Cathcart, too, was in the room. Much to Violet's and Jenny's amazement, she had volunteered to sit with Becca so that Violet could get some rest. They learned that underneath all of her pretension was a kind and generous woman. She spoke up. "Mr. Moses," she said, "the doctor comes to see Becca every day. He's a university graduate, and he keeps up with the latest medicines. Please believe me when I say that Becca is getting the very best care, and between Miss Violet and myself, she has round-the-clock nursing."

"Well …."

"Still, you must be prepared for the worst. Her case is very bad, very difficult to treat. She may not recover," Mrs. Cathcart added kindly. "Please speak with your son about it."

"Well ...."

"Would you like us to pray for Becca?" Violet asked.

"I'll do it myself," he said, stretching to his full height. And so he did—on and on and on, ending with an earsplitting A-MEN! Becca was alert enough to roll her eyes, and Violet quickly ushered him out of the room.

~~~

Becca was buried on the plantation where she was born and grew up, worked, married, and gave birth. Preacher Horne, from Starke's Chapel A.M.E. Church delivered the sermon at graveside, winding himself up to a high-fevered pitch with his preaching and pacing, while the local folks blew gnats off their sweaty faces and Jenny and Violet stood swatting.

Jenny was glad the ushers had finally closed the casket, putting a stop to the endless parading. She did not like seeing her beloved Becca all crinkly and stiff like an old washboard.

She looked around at those gathered. There were whites, coloreds, and in-betweens—the ones Becca had called "high yallers," though she'd said most of those had moved away to live a white life. Old (Holy) Moses was there groaning loudly and grieving his best, as was expected. Young Moses stood quietly to one side, the saddest young man Jenny had ever remembered seeing. In the distance one could hear the occasional faint sound of the tolling church bell.

When Preacher Horne finally gasped his last sentence—"Praise God, Hallelujah, and A-men!"—the choir began singing "Walking in the Light," and the mourners joined in, swaying from side to side. Jenny hoped this was the end, because her feet were swelling in their patent leather slippers, and the chemise under her mourning dress was sticking to her body.

But the end was not yet. "Now we come to the time," droned Preacher Horne, "when friends are invited to say a few words about our dear departed one, to pay their las' respec's. Who will be first?"

Jenny groaned inwardly.

"That's me," answered one of the high yallers. "I knowed Becca Weaver from the time we was chillun together. Come from a long line o' weavers, she did, an' that's where she got her name. Her mam, ol' Sarah Weaver, was the best weaver 'round these parts. Why, her fingers flew so fast you couldn' see which way they was a-goin'. Becca could weave too, only not so good as her mam. She tried, yes she did."

An old man spoke up, at least Jenny thought he was old. She really could not tell. He had a wad of snuff laid back in his jaw, which made his mouth look funny when he talked. "Seems like when ol' Sarah passed away, Becca didn' want to work on the plantation no mo'," he said, scratching at his gray, curly hair. "She'd already seen her daddy sweat hisself to death workin' long hours in the hot sun, so she got herself a job in the tobacco factory other side o' town." The old man spat on the ground. "Spunky, she was. Made a dollar a week stemming tobacco! That was afore she married Ol' Moses." Holy Moses moaned loudly.

Then a young girl spoke. "What I liked best 'bout Becca was that she was so smart. She learned to read an' write. An' she read to us girls and boys and made us happy."

"She was smart, all right," said the old man. "Smart enough not to tell the white fo'ks she could read!" The crowd chuckled low over that.

When the "words" were finished, Becca's casket was lowered into the ground, and her friends decorated it with pieces of broken pitchers, bits of colored glass, and the last item she had used—her stirring spoon—as was the custom. Finally, a patchwork quilt was laid on top. Two men were chosen to fill in the grave with dirt, and the crowd dispersed. But not to go home.

The next stop was over a rutted dirt road to Granny Lizzie's shotgun house (called that because you could look in the front door and see straight through and out the back door, like a shot). There the mourners would find food and celebration—not of death, but of Becca Weaver's *life*.

The house, made of weathered gray wood, had pretty wisteria creeping up its sides. It was small, and Jenny wondered how there would be room for everyone. On the front porch, which ran the length of the house, were cane fishing poles, some wooden barrels and a pick axe. Inside were wooden washtubs, turned upside-down for seating; two rocking chairs, each covered with a homemade quilt; a butter churn; and shelves lined with old whiskey jugs. There were people in every one of the four rooms and spilling into the back yard. Jenny and Violet were speechless with amazement. They had never been in such a poor—yet warm and friendly—place.

Granny Lizzie wasn't Becca's granny, or anyone else's that anyone knew of, but that's what everyone called her. She had covered the table in her biggest room with oilcloth and spread it with cornbread, homemade pork sausages, and sweet-potato pie. A huge black pot hanging over the fire in the wide fireplace was full of dumplings swimming in rich gravy. Granny Lizzie was known for putting on big "to-do's," and Becca Weaver's family and friends would get nothing but the best. Expense wasn't much of a concern, because Becca had religiously saved her money for just such a send-off.

Everyone clapped their hands and sang "I'll Fly Away," and Jenny and Violet were able to sing too, because they had learned it from Becca herself. Granny Lizzie watched them with her toothless grin and told Violet when it was over that she was glad Becca's white folks weren't the uppity kind.

Then a wonderful thing happened, something that made Jenny forget all about her tight shoes and sticky chemise. Some of the young Negro men and women in the back yard began dancing the Juba— patting their hands on their knees and shoulders in intricate configurations that moved so swiftly that limbs seemed to be flying everywhere, unattached to the rest of their bodies. Jenny was entranced. Fascinated! She wanted to know how they did it! Without thinking, she took a sudden step toward Young Moses, but Violet in her wisdom placed a gentle, restraining hand on her arm.

"Not now, Jenny," she said, knowing exactly what was on her young charge's mind.

Jenny smiled. Of course Violet was right. She would ask Young Moses later, after his grief had subsided. She would not forget, either, because she intended to incorporate some of that Juba into her own dancing. Her own limbs would fly like the wings of birds! Onstage. In front of an audience. It would be spectacular!

Before taking their leave, Violet quietly counseled Jenny on the proper way to console Young Moses, who had been standing in a corner by himself. As they approached him, Old Moses joined them.

After the required preliminaries, Young Moses said softly, "I'm not jes' sad. I'm worried somethin' awful."

"Is it something we can help you with?" Violet offered.

"No, Ma'am. It's jes' that … well, what if she ain't really dead?"

"What?"

"What I mean is … it'd be jes' awful if she's down there under all that dirt and cain't get out."

Jenny found herself at a loss for words.

"Young Moses," Violet said, gently. "Becca passed away several days ago. Surely, if she were alive, she would have awakened before this."

"I don' know," he said, shaking his head back and forth. "I heard tell o' folks bein' buried alive. Kinfolk opened their coffins and found scratch marks on the top, or the bodies had turned over."

"Becca was embalmed, wasn't she?"

"No, Ma'am!" said Old Moses, taking charge. "Only the ointments what's needed to preserve her skin. I don' hold with no body-tamperin'." He turned to his son. "I was worried 'bout that same thing, but the Lord God Almighty tol' me in a dream what to do. He tol' me to do the same as what my ma done for my pa, an' I did." Old Moses laid a kind, well-intentioned hand on his son's shoulder. "I put a crowbar an' a small shovel under yo' mama's body, so she kin git out if she's a mind to."

There was nothing more to be said.

~~~

Late that night, Jenny lay sleepless in her four-poster, feeling sadness and loss. Even the tick-tock of the clock seemed to say, "Becca's gone, Becca's gone …."

Then she suddenly realized another terrible thing: Becca had died too soon … without telling Jenny where she had taken Evelette.

Chapter 19

Though she let Young Moses grieve for just two weeks before insisting he teach her the Juba, Jenny allowed two months before asking him about her child.

"I don' know, Miz Jenny. I don' know nothin' 'bout that baby." His eyes were respectfully downcast.

"Young Moses, my parents are dead now; your mother is gone, God rest her soul; and I want my child! There is no reason on this earth why I should not have her back!" Jenny's voice rose with desperation. She was beyond gentleness, beyond diplomacy. "Where did you take her?" she shouted.

But Young Moses held his ground. "I didn' take her nowheres, Miz Jenny. I'm tellin' you the same as I tol' that pretty lady what visited a while back. I don' know where that baby is."

"Don't lie to me!"

Defying custom, Young Moses raised his head and looked Jenny squarely in the eyes. "Back then, when Mama had two days off," he said, slowly, "she took the baby from yo' house to Granny Lizzie's. Sometime during the first night, she slipped away wif the baby, and came back wifout it. My mama was the only one who knowed where she took that baby." He held his breath for a long time, then let it out in a heavy sigh. "That's God's truth."

And Jenny knew it was.

~~~

Evelette was dead. At least she was dead to Jenny, for there was nowhere else to turn. The only other person who might have a clue would be Granny Lizzie, but Becca would not have confided in her. During the times when Becca had told Jenny stories of her life on the plantation, she'd said more than once that Granny Lizzie had never kept a secret in her life! Outside of searching the face of every dark-haired little girl she saw on the streets for resemblance to Tyler or herself, Jenny had no further recourse. And if she kept looking at faces, and wondering, and worrying … she would go mad! Sometimes she thought she already had.

When Jenny Alcott finally convinced herself that Evelette was dead—because it was the only way she could go on living—she, too, died in a figurative sense. Because that was the moment when Alissa Jennings was born to take her place.

~~~

Andrea immediately noticed the difference in the written entries, which became fewer. The spontaneous, natural flow of the young teenager was suddenly more polished, more manufactured, as if it were written for an audience rather than for personal release and comfort. The signature, too, was worth noting.

… Several jaunts have been scheduled to neighboring cities, where I shall ply my craft. And I am to entertain for yet another grand soiree at the Mitchell House Hotel tonight. They simply cannot seem to get enough of me. Nor can I get enough of dancing—not just dancing, but dancing for audiences, talking with audiences. Everyone I meet is my audience! Can I help it if they expect me to respond as an entertainer?
Alissa

~~~

It was true. Everyone became her audience—the grocer, the milliner, the neighbors, even the church's congregation, though they were not too happy about her chosen occupation. Just a year before, the church board had reprimanded their assistant organist for attending the "germons" in one of the town's hotels. The germons were elaborate social dances, and the church did not approve. So what were they to do with their financially faithful member, Alissa Jennings, who flitted and flirted onstage, twisting her body into all sorts of unspeakable contortions?

"Be glad you weren't at services last Sunday, Jenny," the young organist confided. "Our young people were scolded royally for desecrating the Sabbath by playing whist, reading dime novels and going to the dance halls."

"Well, the church seems to tolerate me," Alissa said.

"That's because you are a professional entertainer," she replied. "And you don't attend services too terribly often, which may be to your advantage." Her eyes twinkled. "You are a curiosity, Jenny-Alissa. That's what you are. And they cannot let go of you."

Alissa laughed. "Or my contributions?"

The only one who wasn't swept up by Alissa Jennings' magic broom was Violet.

"I am not sure all this business is such a good idea," Violet said late one afternoon. Alissa had just returned from a long session with her dance teacher and was sprawled on the four-poster, fanning herself. Violet sat crocheting in a straight-back, padded chair near the bed.

"What business?"

"This ... Alissa Jennings business."

"What about it?"

"I don't know. It just seems so ... false, somehow."

The younger woman kept fanning herself, her eyes closed. "It is what I have always wanted, Aunt Violet," she said. "And, if you remember, it is what you wanted for me. You told me to dream dreams, to reach for the stars, to work hard and achieve. You said that."

"Yes, dear. I know I did. And I still want you to do that—to build a life on your most attainable dreams. But I think you are carrying it a little too far, and perhaps too fast. Your Alissa character is just that—a character, as shallow as water on a cookie sheet. She is not only on the stage these days. She is everywhere. She is on the sidewalk, in the store, at church. Much to my dismay, she 'held court' last week under the Big Oak!"

A low, throaty chuckle emitted from behind the fan.

"Alissa is even at home," Violet said, quietly.

The chuckle became a heavy sigh, and Violet continued, "Like right now. That was Alissa's sigh. Alissa is impatient with me."

The young woman on the bed stopped fanning and opened her eyes. "Aunt Violet, I am sorry if this bothers you. Truly, I'm sorry. But I am changing. I *have* changed. That does not mean, though, that my feelings about you have changed." She propped herself up on one elbow. "You have always been my closest friend, my dearest relative, my favorite person in the whole world, and you always will be. I love you dearly, I really do. But now it's Alissa Jennings who loves you, because I … am … Alissa … Jennings!"

Violet remained tranquil. "No, dear. You pretend to be, but you are not. Alissa Jennings doesn't exist outside of your imagination. You are Jenny Alcott."

The response was kind but firm. "Not anymore."

~~~

With her new identity came new clothing—more functional (and more eye-catching, since it was a step outside of current fashion)— and a new hairstyle. Gone was the simple, tied-back-with-a-ribbon look, and in its place was the popular "psyche knot"—hair pulled straight back from the face and knotted on top. Alissa was considered eccentric, but delightfully so, since everyone liked her immensely.

The bedazzled young church organist put it very well when she confided to Alissa one day, "If you had come from somewhere like New York or Boston, depending on your attitude and demeanor, the townfolk might not have had anything to do with you. But you didn't.

You arrived from the cultured city of far-off London as Jenny Alcott; yet, in a sense, you were born here—at least Alissa was. So you are *theirs*. Ours! That makes all the difference."

Violet watched her niece's inward and outward changes with dismay … and enormous guilt. She felt responsible for the direction Jenny's life had taken and, in a remorseful way, told her that. Alissa, of course, pooh-poohed the idea, saying she, herself, was responsible. She had done exactly as she had wanted, and had not her life turned out *marvelous*?

"It isn't marvelous to me," said Violet. "First Tyler and the baby, then your father's heart failure and subsequent death, not to mention your mother's fatal accident, which probably happened because she was distracted with worry. Now this … this Alissa creature."

"Creature?"

"All along, I have encouraged, even taken part in, your adventures. Now, I am not so sure I did the right thing. I am not very happy with the end result."

"You are not happy with me?" Alissa asked, and Violet caught a brief glimpse of Jenny.

"I'm happy with *you*, dear. It is Alissa that I'm not happy with, and I feel responsible."

Alissa managed a wry smile. "Do you worry that you have created a monster? Perhaps similar to the one in Mary Shelley's novel?"

Violet sighed in exasperation, then shook her head fiercely to banish the horrible analogy.

"Just remember, I love you," Alissa said, kissing her aunt lightly on the forehead.

~~~

More and more, Violet began to withdraw, not from what she considered to be the "old" Jenny in masquerade—never from her beloved niece—but from society in general. This worried Alissa, but not enough for her to change the way she lived.

Violet, therefore, turned her full attention to running the house.

Fortunately, she had persuaded Young Moses to move into Becca's rooms above the carriage house, and he was grateful to be working full time on his own, away from Old Moses. Although another cook-housekeeper had been hired after Becca died, she was a day worker who only came three times a week. Violet soon made the woman responsible for shopping and errands, which left her with little excuse to go outside. She had little interest in eating, and, as a result, was losing weight. She no longer returned social calls, and, though she liked to walk, she seldom ventured further than the block on which she lived. Oddly, she missed the days when she and Jenny had enjoyed bicycling up and down Dawson Street. Alissa had no time for that now, and Violet had no desire to go alone.

The only place Violet found social contact—and a sense of peace—was at church. And the *only* one in whom she confided was God.

This preoccupation with prayer disturbed Alissa even more than Violet's withdrawal. She longed for the old, easy rapport, when the two of them could talk about anything and everything. Sometimes she tried, but it was not easy for her anymore, either, and it seemed that Violet had lost the ability to relax. She knew that her aunt was waiting for the old Jenny Alcott to appear. But that simply was not going to happen.

~~~

Alissa Jennings had wasted no time weaving bits and pieces of the Juba dance into her routine. In fact, she thought of it as exactly that—weaving, much as Old Sarah must have woven her cotton. With that as inspiration, she named her new dance "The Weave."

Like fingers across a loom, her hands, arms, feet and legs flew in, across, and out of the Juba movements, and in between she wound and unwound her thread—her body—in slow, sultry twists and turns. The white folks who watched Alissa perform did not know about Juba movements or where they came from (or if they suspected, they did not admit it). Rather, they discussed the way Miss Jennings "played with the rhythm sequences in her music." That made it all right.

Because audiences enjoyed and expected it, The Weave became Alissa Jennings' signature dance, as scarf-dancing had distinguished Loie Fuller. It brought her fame ... and also notoriety. It established her identity as someone who dared to be different.

~~~

It was here that Alissa's entries stopped abruptly. Andrea reached behind her back and adjusted the pillows, propping herself a little higher. Briefly, she massaged her neck, then looked closely at the next several pages.

All that remained were a few fragile newspaper clippings about Alissa Jennings' successes and escapades, and an occasional souvenir program ... until Andrea came across the final, lengthy entry in another handwriting. She looked ahead and saw that it had been signed, "Violet Alcott."

Chapter 20

... so I keep the few things she sends me. I believe this is the appropriate place to put them. I do not care to look at them again. I shall always love Jenny, but I do not like Alissa very much—this torments me!

I shall try to record what has come to pass in the last years. I am not sure why I'm doing this. Perhaps because I know that Jenny will not. I am quite certain that she will not return to the attic studio—she has shown no interest in it for several years—and I am absolutely certain that she will never again lift the floorboards and remove the diaries. The reason? Because she is Alissa Jennings (or thinks she is) and Alissa hasn't the need that Jenny had.

What is my need? The same as Jenny's was in the beginning—catharsis. Nothing else. I cannot imagine who would ever be interested in reading these pages. Or why. Though I pray daily that my true Jenny will return before I die, I know in my heart of hearts that it will not happen. "Oh ye of little faith?" Yes. I pray a lot, but nothing ever comes of it.

Did I create a monster? No, not a monster, but certainly something other than what I expected. There was a time—as

*a young girl, a young woman—when I would have envied
Jenny's life. God forgive me, perhaps I still do!* ...

~~~

In the spring of 1895, Governor William McKinley of Ohio met
with leaders of the Republican party in a rented house on Dawson
Street, just four blocks from the Alcott home. They were there to
plan the Governor's campaign for the Presidency. During that time,
a large reception was given and many townspeople were invited,
including Violet Alcott. She did not attend. Governor McKinley went
to services each Sunday morning at the Methodist Episcopal Church.
But Violet did not see him there, either, as she even had stopped
attending her beloved church.

Because the local "air" was considered healthy, more people were
visiting the area and many were staying. Most were wealthy and
influential northerners, and many were descendants of earlier
plantation owners—those who had seen fit to raise money for a
railroad many years before. Though repairs had to be made after the
Civil War, the Savannah, Florida, and Western Railroad maintained
a line from Savannah on the east to Albany on the west, making
travel relatively easy to and from the pretty little Georgia town that
Alissa Jennings called home. Dazzled by the prospects presented by
the combination of healthy air and a good railroad, the local citizenry
began promoting Thomasville as a major resort and made the pages
of a popular new book by Morris Phillips, *Abroad and at Home.*

For Alissa, the timing was perfect. Hotels sprouted up like glorious
flowering weeds, and social functions requiring entertainment
abounded. There were festive parties, such as the "Pink Tea and
Wheelbarrow Reception" given by the ladies of the city at Courthouse
Park. Guests were asked to come "in the spirit of pinkness." And
who was rolled in, making a grand entrance perched on a pink
wheelbarrow? ... Alissa Jennings, in breathtaking pink chiffon!

She took advantage of every opportunity, whether or not it required
dancing. It was important to be "seen." She was seen at the

Watermelon Carnival in Paradise Park, the Thanksgiving Day football game, at an outing with the Turks Base Ball Team, and at the opening of the new Glen Arven golf course.

With increased demand for her presence, Alissa was no longer able to take regular lessons from Catherine Kingsley. The two remained friends, however, and, as a superb gesture of friendship, Miss Kingsley began functioning as Alissa's agent. Because the train made travel so accessible, Alissa's first long-distance booking was easy—The Savannah Theatre. What excitement!

"Oh, *please* come with me, Violet!" Alissa had stopped addressing her as "aunt." Her eyes were bright and clear, and Violet saw flecks of Jenny within them.

"Me?" she asked, surprised.

"Of course you! You have not seen me dance for a long, long time, and you have never seen The Weave all put together."

"But I've watched you rehearse."

"That is not the same. You haven't seen me in my costume and makeup, or under the lights. There is something *marvelous* about performing under the lights. Please come with me … it will be like old times."

As Alissa (who at this moment sounded more like Jenny) spoke, Violet felt a long-forgotten, youthful energy surging within her own body. From earlier times as an eager young theatre enthusiast, she recalled the smell of the stage and the heat of the lights. Remembering myriad theatre outings with Jenny, she could picture the audience, the rush of the crowd, hear the applause. Suddenly, she felt a burden lifting from her frail limbs, as if it were fleeing on wings, and she answered, "Yes, dear. Yes! I shall go with you to Savannah!"

~~~

The train ride itself was an adventure. They traveled in a first-class compartment, furthest from the bumps and jolts of the wheels, and it was extremely comfortable. The sofa-type seats were richly upholstered with thick padding and scarlet damask, and the walls were made of magnificently detailed woodwork. Since they traveled on Sunday, Violet was especially pleased that the gathering car had a pump organ, so the travelers could join together in the Sunday hymns.

The Savannah Theatre on Chippewa Square was much more opulent than the Thomasville Opera House in which she (as Jenny) had debuted. It reminded Violet more of The Empire back home in London, where she and Jenny had gone to see Loie Fuller and, unfortunately, where Jenny had met Tyler Fleming. While Alissa rehearsed, Violet wandered the corridors and explored the backstage area, inhaling the grandeur, as if it were possible, and allowing the excitement of anticipation to swell within.

"Oh, I cannot wait!" Alissa cried on the afternoon of her performance.

"You shall have to, if you want an audience in those seats," Violet replied.

Alissa giggled, like the old Jenny. She was working on Violet's hair. Though Violet's gown was modest, she had given Alissa permission to twist her hair out of its familiar chignon and into a psyche knot.

"Did you see my photographs on the placards out front?"

"Of course, dear. How could I miss them? I have been over every inch of this building."

"What did you think?"

"Of your photographs or the building?"

Alissa poked her aunt good-naturedly. "You! Of course I mean my photographs!"

Of course she did. Alissa was self-absorbed. Violet had noticed the subtle changes. As Alissa grew and Jenny shrank, her interest in other people dwindled, except as they could be used to further her career. It was sad. Doubly so, because Violet did not honestly object to what Alissa was *doing* ... but to what she was *becoming*.

"Your photographs are lovely, dear."

"You mean glamorous!"

"That, too."

"Well, you are going to be glamorous tonight. There! Look in the glass and tell me what you think."

Violet held up the small mirror and peeked at her image, watching as her whole face came alive with laughter. "Is it really me?" she asked.

"It *is* you, and you are beautiful. You look like a young girl again."

She did. It was amazing, because over the past months she had noticed visible signs of aging. She had grieved a bit for her youth but had given in to the inevitable, taking less interest and less care in her appearance.

There was more to it than that, though. She had agreed to this adventure, knowing something that Alissa did not—that it would be her last. Part of her aging was due to her decline in health. She had finally gathered the courage to ask Dr. Ainsworth about the small cluster of globular tumors on the side of her abdomen and was dismayed to learn that nothing could be done for them … or for her.

That was the catalyst that finally made her decide to take this trip, determined to live every moment to the hilt. It would be the time of her life, at the end of her life.

What pleasure Violet took in Alissa's performance! Her niece certainly was *marvelous*—flawless, captivating, entrancing, enchanting … and even a bit risqué. Violet knew that she should purse her lips in disapproval of those immodest sequences, but she could not. She smiled brightly and laughed inwardly at the antics she would have loved to indulge in herself. The trip to Savannah was truly a highlight of her life.

When they arrived home, the train station was filled with people coming and going; but there also was a group of Alissa's loyal young followers who had come solely to greet her. They waved and cheered and held out pencils and scraps of paper for her to write her name. She had everyone's attention and she basked in it.

~~~

During those early years as Alissa, only one woman briefly

overshadowed her in Thomasville, and that was Annie Oakley, who stormed in with Buffalo Bill's Wild West Show in 1899.

Alissa, at twenty-three, thought Annie (who was thirty-nine but looked ten years younger) was awfully old to be getting so much attention. The odd thing was that photographs of Annie in her twenties, with long dark hair and piercing eyes, bore a striking resemblance to Alissa. Annie was not nearly as thin and graceful, but she struck the same kind of posture—setting her chin proudly, as if she dared anyone to challenge the life she had chosen.

Her presence made Alissa distinctly uncomfortable. Compared to Annie Oakley, who was idolized all over the world, Alissa Jennings was a mere fledgling. When the popular entertainer appeared on Broad Street one afternoon, crowds gathered around her, ignoring Alissa who stood only a few yards away.

"She can even shoot from a bicycle and from horseback!" exclaimed a young man as he pushed past.

"In her fringed buckskin dresses and men's hats!" Alissa yelled back through the noise. But Violet was the only one who heard.

For Alissa, Annie Oakley's visit was both good and bad. It put her in her place, but it also strengthened her resolve to achieve. Jenny Alcott's dream was to become a great dancer, but Alissa Jennings had lost sight of that. Alissa's dream was to become famous.

Fortunately, Annie Oakley moved on … and that was what gave Alissa the idea for her next adventure—a tour!

~~~

"Oh, Violet," Alissa said, "it is going to be *marvelous*! I shall be stopping at all the important places, and some not so important, but they shall be adventures, too."

"You've chosen a hard life, dear, going from station to station. Don't they call it playing to the whistle stops?"

"That is not what I have in mind. I want to tour Europe, like Annie Oakley did—England, France, Spain, Italy, Austria, Hungary, Germany. I want the whole world to know who Alissa Jennings is!"

"Whistle stops."

"Violet, think of me as a … a butterfly, flitting from one blossom to another."

Violet chuckled.

"Would you consider coming with me?" Alissa asked. "I would love to have you along on the tour."

Her aunt smiled sadly and said, "No, dear. I do not 'flit' very well these days. I am afraid it would be too much for an old woman like me."

"You are not old! If anyone has the spirit of eternal youth, you do." She tilted her head with a sly smile and said, "I saw you last Sunday—riding with those other ladies in the doctor's new red Cadillac!"

Violet had the grace to blush. "'The spirit is willing but the flesh is weak,'" she quoted. "I must take that literally. My flesh is weak indeed—much too weak to go on a tour. Perhaps I can join you later," she added, knowing full well that "later" would never come.

Alissa seemed satisfied with that.

The following month she went off on her tour, and the clippings and programs began coming home to Violet.

Alissa Jennings never did come home to Violet.

~~~

"I know that Jenny loves me," Violet wrote, nearing the end of her entry in the diary. "I know she does. She will see that I get a proper burial. I want to be buried here in Laurel Hill Cemetery, not in London. London is not my home anymore, just as this is not Jenny's home anymore. I know why she doesn't come back. It is too painful. She remembers Evelette, even though she says the child is dead. Saying it—that doesn't make it so. I often heard her crying in the night."

Violet's penmanship was showing deterioration, and Andrea had difficulty reading the last few pages. Some of it was disjointed and didn't make a great deal of sense. Noticeable, too, was that from this point on, Violet referred to her niece as Jenny—never again as Alissa.

I mourn for Evelette, I mourn for Jenny, and I mourn for my lost self. It is sad that the time really does come when it is too late. You cannot go back and do it all over again. It is just ... too ... late.

I wish I had lived in a time when things were different. I wish that women were as important as men, that women who have intelligence could use it and not have to pretend, feigning innocence and ignorance just to make men feel important. There is something wrong with that. I wish that women's opinions counted for something—that women were not sent to the withdrawing room when important matters were discussed.

"I shall leave a list of instructions," she wrote, "and I'll explain to Jenny why I have chosen to sell this house, which she has given me for my own. Mr. and Mrs. Norman Cooper have agreed to buy it."

Andrea gasped. Her great-grandparents had bought the house directly from Violet Alcott! Now she felt even more connected to this long-ago family.

Violet apparently had left her affairs in good order. She talked about having the furniture picked up and distributed to needy people after her death—except for the four-poster that had belonged to Jenny. She wanted it left in the house, and Mr. and Mrs. Cooper had agreed to keep it there.

"It is very special," she wrote, "because it was Jenny's retreat when times were difficult. It is where Evelette was born ... and it is where I shall die."

She was adamant about leaving the bed in the house, and she hoped that it would always stay there. "I feel within my heart that if her bed remains in the house, the spirit of the real Jenny Alcott will remain here too. ... Jenny did not leave when Alissa did. She couldn't have. Perhaps one day my darling Jenny will find peace. The wedding handkerchief that I crocheted for her while we were yet in London is inside the southwest bedpost. She will never use it. Nor will I."

The ink of the final page was tear-stained and smeared:

> ... *I have tried to lead a good life insofar as possible, given my natural inclination toward wantonness.*
>
> *For too many years I have struggled with this internal paradox—wanting to do right, yet desiring what is wrong. Even now, I wish (for the wrong reason) that I had married— not because I long for children of my own (which I do), but because ... because I regret never knowing what it feels like to have a man between my legs. ... God forgive me! If I had married my Samuel, it would have been a beautiful union of two loving bodies, not something dirty and evil, no matter what "they" say.*
>
> *I am trying to explain to myself why I was never able to condemn Jenny for stretching the outer limits of propriety, for tasting the pleasures of the flesh, for seeking personal fame and fortune. Perhaps some day (though I am sure it would take a hundred years or more), what is considered "right" for men will no longer be considered "wrong" for women. Oh, that I could live so long!*
>
> *Alas, it is not to be. My strength is failing, my limbs are tired. I shall not climb these stairs again. Therefore, whatever remains of my wasted life, or of Jenny Alcott's (if she still exists within, or outside of, Alissa Jennings) shall go unrecorded ... except such as the Almighty sees fit to include in the Book of Heaven.*
>
> *Violet Alcott*

~~~

Andrea swallowed hard. Her mouth was dry and her eyes were wet with tears. Violet's letter had touched her as much, or more, than anything Jenny had written. She could almost hear the woman's inner wailing—still pent-up, straining at the bonds of silence as she neared the last days of her "wasted" life. How tragic—to have so much inner beauty, intelligence, personality, love and, above all, *worth* ... yet be unable to share it except in the most basic ways. The most accepted ways. Worse yet, to believe that what little she had shared of herself had corrupted someone else. ... No wonder she'd looked upon her life as wasted. She had never allowed herself to live.

Suddenly, it occurred to Andrea that Jenny had never recorded Violet's feelings about the loss of Evelette. Yet, there they were at the end of the diary—years of suppressed pain bursting out in four poignant words: "I mourn for Evelette."

"I, too, mourn for Evelette," Andrea said aloud. At that moment the familiar sense of *déjà vu* brushed over her body, light as a feather, as if Evelette's fate were somehow entwined in her own ... and the curtain did its now-familiar, now-comforting flutter.

Andrea climbed off the bed and inspected the bedposts. *The wedding handkerchief is in the southwest post. Which one would that be?* She started at the foot of the bed, pulling and twisting at the pineapple on top of the first post. It moved! She turned it with more pressure and it came off with a sharp squeak. Without hesitation she reached inside the shallow opening and retrieved the exquisite piece of needlework. It was beautifully preserved.

"You're not going back into that hole," she said aloud to the handkerchief. "I'm going to put you in a frame, protect you with glass, and display you in open view to remind me every day of the value of Alex's love in my life. I am so much more fortunate than either of you were—Dear Violet, Dear Jenny."

Had she become so absorbed with this family that she was thinking of them as if they were still alive? She could remember times past, when she had been engrossed in a really good novel and, at the end, did not want to let the characters go, didn't want the story to end. Well, maybe that's what she was experiencing now. The diaries were sort of like a novel, and she did not want to let the characters go, didn't want their lives to end ... at least not like they had.

Chapter 21

Andrea glanced at her watch. It was far past supper time, but she wasn't hungry, and a little more than two hours still remained before Alex would be home.

Now that she knew *why* Jenny's bed had been left in the house, she was better able to put her own unsettling experiences into perspective. She had never been one to believe in the paranormal, but Violet's statement about Jenny's spirit living on in the house was like a revelation. It had suspended her disbelief. She knew it was so! The certain realization that what she had felt was Jenny's presence not only gave her a sense of anticipation—of what, she didn't yet know—but also a sense of relief. The spirit of Jenny Alcott was not something to fear.

At the moment, Andrea's body ached from being in one position for such a long time. Her brain was tired, too.

Suddenly, she remembered and spoke aloud: "Becca's Apple Pie!" She glanced at her watch one more time and made the decision. She wouldn't wait until tomorrow to bake it. Out of the four-poster, down the stairs and into the kitchen she went. This would be a great way to use up some of the half-bushel of apples that one of Alex's clients had brought them from Ellijay, a little "apple" town in the North Georgia mountains.

Andrea was actually singing when she reached for Becca's recipe.

Hurriedly, but carefully, she picked up the fragile, yellowed paper and placed it on the bar under the light. Though the wording was strangely funny, the penmanship was clear. Becca Weaver had been one of the lucky "coloreds," because she had learned to read and write. At the bottom of the recipe she'd written this message:

Pie tastes real good with a cup of coffee, but the plan of buying ground coffee is bad; much of it is mixed with peas, which you can raise for less than 15 or 20 cents a pound and mix for yourself.

Andrea laughed aloud. There was no way she'd put peas in her coffee! Translating the measurements to modern terms wasn't nearly as difficult as she had imagined. In fact, it was fun, and she found herself looking forward to surprising Alex with it. She worked quickly.

When the pies were safely in the oven and the kitchen shining clean once again, she hurried upstairs to wash her hair and take a ten-minute soak in the claw-foot tub. All the while she was making the pies, she'd thought of Violet's lost opportunity and her "desire for what is wrong." She could not get that silent cry out of her mind.

In one respect, at least, she was glad that the "good old days" were gone and that she had Alex. And that she didn't need to play coy little games with him. She loved him, and right now her need for him was overwhelming. She longed for the sound of his voice, the smell of his skin, his embrace, his kisses, his caresses in all the wonderfully erotic places, his … his everything !

She poured rose-scented bubblebath into the tub and laid out the rose-scented body lotion. He'd notice the scent, because it was his favorite. It was light, but definitely discernable. After the bath, she would brush the water from her hair until it was dry and shining, and put on her lacy red negligee—the one that left absolutely nothing to the imagination! She, like Violet, had desire … but she didn't worry for a minute that it was wrong. It was very right!

~~~

Alex picked up his car at the Tallahassee Airport and drove home with as much speed as he dared. This was no time to get caught—he missed his wife and wanted no delays.

I'm more alive *now,* he thought, *more awake to Andrea's needs. I've been too self-satisfied, too unaware. It's no wonder she's been moody. No wonder she hasn't started painting again. There hasn't been much to inspire her—no color in her life.*

His need for her was all-consuming. He longed for the sound of her voice, the sweet scent of her skin, her soft kisses, her knowing touch ... and much, much more. As soon as he got in the door, he would hug her, then kiss her like he'd never kissed her before— longer, deeper, with soft caresses all over her body—enough to make her need for him as great as his was for her. Then, they'd head for the bedroom, never mind the nightclothes.

~~~

The first thing Alex noticed when he entered the kitchen through the back door was the smell of apple pie and roses. ... Roses? He could see the pies on cooling racks on the bar, but where were the roses?

"Andrea?" he called, walking down the hall with his airline bag. "Andrea? Are you here?"

"Alex! I'm upstairs."

He started up the stairs, and as he went, the scent of roses overtook the smell of apple pie. All he had to do was follow his nose—straight to the bathroom door.

Andrea stood naked in front of the full-length mirror, brushing her hair. He couldn't remember when she had looked more beautiful. At nearly forty years old, her curves were still softly defined, her tantalizing breasts gently rounded. Tonight, her skin was glowing. He put his bag on the floor and leaned against the door casing, never taking his eyes from her.

"You're a little early," she said, turning toward him. There was a sly smile on her mouth.

"I think I'm glad." His eyes traveled very slowly over every inch of her body.

She stood still, and as she enjoyed his pleasure, her own became silently obvious.

He looked at her breasts … and his smile grew wider.

"I had planned to put on my red negligee," she said softly.

"Don't you dare," he whispered.

Chapter 22

It wasn't until the next evening, when Alex came home from the office, that Andrea gathered the courage to tell him what had *really* been bothering her. Alex had just given her the gifts he'd brought back from New York and she was feeling especially close to him. She'd been very happy with the gifts, particularly the palette pin with its jeweled splashes of color.

"And this frame, Alex. It's beautiful! I have just the picture to put in it. Wait 'til you see! Oh, Alex, I love you so much. Please forgive me for being so moody these last few weeks. I'm really not unhappy with our new life, nor with *us*."

"You had me a little scared. Oh, hell, I was a *lot* scared."

"The things I said, even that we didn't have any friends here in Thomasville—those were not the reasons I was touchy or grouchy. They were superficial *excuses* for my guilt."

"Andrea, you don't have anything to feel guilty about," Alex said.

"But I do! You just don't know."

"Your mother ruled you with that weapon, and I refuse to be a party to it." He stopped short, remembering his long conversation with himself on the way home from New York. "Unless ... unless you want to tell me."

She snuggled up close to him on the sofa, near tears. "I do and I don't. But mostly I do."

He put his arm around her and pulled her even closer. "Just remember, I love you with all of my heart. I always will, and nothing you tell me will change that."

Tears spilled onto her cheeks as she began telling him about the summer in Paris, when she was eighteen. About Roger Overby. And, finally, about her son and his unfortunate death when her cab was caught in rush-hour traffic on the way to the hospital. "It was my fault, Alex. I waited too long to call the cab. I should have called Aunt Mary. I should have—"

"Stop," he said, gently. "Stop heaping more guilt on yourself. It was not your fault. You were eighteen years old and inexperienced. Now you're almost forty years old and you're my darling wife. I love you."

"But there's more!"

Alex waited quietly.

"The birth and death of my son is the reason I could never have other children, the reason I can never have your child. I never told you that. I only said that I couldn't have children."

"And didn't I accept that? Did I ask why?"

"No." She brushed her tears with her hand. "Do you care?"

"About *why*? No, Andrea, I don't. You are all I want in life, all I need, all I care about. And, frankly, I'm too old for children. I like our life the way it is." He kissed her forehead tenderly and she buried her face in his chest.

"I like it, too, Alex. Very much. Please forgive last week's moods. They were all a smoke screen. Even I didn't realize that this was the problem, the guilt I've felt all these years, especially the guilt of not being honest with you when you first asked me to marry you. I didn't realize it until I started reading the diaries. Jenny had an illegitimate child, too, and her feelings about her child started me thinking about mine. Except her child lived. Jenny never found her, though, after Evelette—that was her daughter—was given away. Jenny never found a man to love her either." Andrea knew she was rambling. She sighed. "But I did find a man to love me." She looked up at him, smiling through her tears.

"You certainly did. Forever and always." Gently and longingly, Alex kissed her, then held her quietly for several moments, as she made peace with her past and with herself.

Finally, Andrea said, "It's so sad that Jenny never found her daughter. Reading about that, in her own words and in her Aunt Violet's words, nearly broke my heart."

"So, when do we start?" he asked.

"Start what?"

"Our search for Evelette."

~~~

Andrea was absolutely glowing! It seemed that she and Alex were more in love than ever, and she could hardly believe that he was actually helping her find Evelette. She had known, deep down inside, that it was something she wanted to do, something she *must* do, for herself as well as for Jenny, but she hadn't recognized it as reality until Alex made the suggestion.

For the next few evenings, she filled him in on the Alcott family—Barclay, Millicent, Violet and Jenny.

"But best of all, Alex, guess what?" (He knew she didn't really want him to guess.) "Jenny Alcott did become famous! She changed her name to—are you ready for this?—Alissa Jennings!"

"You're kidding."

"No, it's true! She was Alissa Jennings!"

Alex was almost speechless—almost. "I've heard my parents talk about her. My grandmother, in fact, said she 'didn't quite know what to make of her.' ... In our attic?" He smiled. "No kidding."

Andrea's eyes were sparkling. "My great-grandparents bought this house directly from Violet Alcott." She looked straight at him. "Do you understand what I'm saying?"

"I'm beginning to."

She took a big breath. "I want to start by visiting Violet's grave," Andrea said. "She was buried right here in town, in Laurel Hill cemetery."

~~~

After finding a plot layout at the city's public works department and locating the grave on it, they went to the cemetery near the downtown area (which in Violet's day would have been on the "outskirts") and walked on the stone pathways to the back corner. It was about 6:30 in the evening and the sun was still shining, though low in the sky, casting pretty shadows among the gravestones. In just a few minutes they stood before a lonely grave under the shadow of a nearby pecan tree. The headstone was plain but had been well cut. It read:

Violet Gwendolyn Alcott
1860-1901
Jenny's dear aunt and dearest friend.

"She came back, Alex. ... *Jenny*—not Alissa—came back to Violet! She would have had the headstone made. Oh, I wonder if she got here before Violet died. Violet wanted so much to see the real Jenny again. Do you suppose that Alissa allowed Jenny to surface from this point on?"

"I doubt it. At least not often. You know what the publicity was like on Alissa Jennings far into the twentieth century. The overused word was 'spectacular,' and she kept the illusion going long after she had stopped dancing."

"I believe Violet was right when she suggested that Jenny's spirit remained in the house, *our* house, while Alissa was busy with 'whistle stops.' I feel her presence, Alex. I really do ... and I am going to find her child."

~~~

While Alex was busy at the office, Andrea was busy at the city library, at the historical society's small museum and at the civil records office. She guessed that the baby had grown up in the area.

Jenny had seemed sure that she was close by. All she had to go on was the name "Evelette"—which appeared absolutely nowhere—and the date of birth, January 1, 1893.

At the records office she discovered that four girl babies were born on that date, and the first, Abigail Maureen Chambers, won a prize for being the "New Year's Baby." The second was Charity Faith Maxwell; the third was simply Vivian Doyle; and the fourth was Hannah Moore. No middle names for the last two. That seemed a good place to start.

Checking the marriage and death records, she found that Hannah Moore, unmarried, had died of "a bilious fever" at age thirty-eight; but Vivian Doyle had married Mr. Charlie O'Brien and lived to celebrate her 100th birthday! She had died in August 1993. Andrea was excited, knowing that her next stop would be the local newspaper archives. Surely in 1993, if someone reached age 100, that would be "news" for a small-town paper!

~~~

Andrea was made comfortable in a room at the *Times-Enterprise* and provided with papers from January and August 1993, which should cover the 100th birthday and the obituary, she thought. She took a deep breath and began reading.

January 1 had fallen on a Friday that year, and it was in the following Monday's paper, January 4, that she found Vivian Doyle O'Brien's 100th birthday celebration noted. It was a very nice article, really, with a photograph. Mrs. O'Brien stood proudly in profile on a grassy lawn. Leaning slightly forward on a sturdy cane, her face was tilted heavenward. Her hair was gray, her skin old and withered.

Andrea was somewhat disappointed but quickly scolded herself. What had she expected? A picture resembling the young Jenny Alcott? The face of Jenny in a 100-year-old woman?

She read the article carefully, looking for clues. There was no mention of the name "Evelette." It did say that Vivian was a resident of Azalea Terrace Life Care Center. Andrea knew that the home was still operational, because she had seen it on the north side of town. The article also made no mention of surviving children or other family, except for her parents, "the late Mr. and Mrs. Harold Doyle." *Is this woman Evelette or not?* she asked herself.

Turning to the August obituaries, she again found Vivian Doyle O'Brien, with no survivors. "As a child she attended church in the Spring Hill community with her parents, the late Harold and Annabelle Doyle. Burial will be in the Spring Hill Church cemetery."

Andrea sighed, closed the papers and looked at her notes. Not much to go on. *This person may not even be Evelette.*

Next stop: Azalea Terrace Life Care Center. She knew she didn't have a prayer of getting to see any records, but she hoped that someone would at least talk with her about Vivian O'Brien.

"Is there anything in Mrs. O'Brien's file that would indicate whether she had a middle name?"

The administrator, Miss Adams, who probably had been a high school student in 1993, was very gracious, but she had not known Mrs. O'Brien; and, no, there was no mention of a middle name. "According to this," she said, looking through the file, "she had only one visitor during the whole time she was here, other than the ladies from her church, that is. That seems odd. Someone from out of state."

"Do you have the name?"

Miss Adams shook her head. "Our records back then weren't thorough, as they are now," she said. "There's no name written down." She paused, thinking. "You know, Mrs. O'Brien's friend, Martha Newsome, still lives here," she offered. "She's ninety-eight years old. Probably won't be much help."

The young administrator led Andrea to a comfortable sofa in the "gathering room" and brought Martha Newsome to her. Mrs. Newsome was a tiny woman with curious eyes and a slightly off-kilter wig. She walked with short, choppy steps, and though she moved quickly, she covered almost no ground. Andrea waited patiently.

After introductions were made and Martha Newsome was seated, Miss Adams excused herself and Andrea began her careful task of quizzing the lady.

"I want to talk with you about your friend, Vivian O'Brien."

Mrs. Newsome's face brightened. "Called me Little Sister, she did. Lots older than me." Then she shook her head. "Such a long time ago."

"Do you know if she had another name?"

"Just Vivian O'Brien."

"What about a second name?" She waited, but the woman didn't respond. "Vivian ... something ... O'Brien?"

"Oh. Let's see ... Boil. Or Toil ... Doil. That's it." She smiled proudly, showing false teeth just a shade too yellow. "Vivian Doyle O'Brien."

"But Doyle is a surname."

"Maiden name. Grew up Vivian Doyle." Martha Newsome had a habit of dropping her pronouns.

"Did she have a middle name? Like ... like Jane, or Edna, or...?" Andrea was probing, but she did not want to plant Evelette's name in the old woman's mind.

Mrs. Newsome thought for a few moments. "Not that she ever said."

"What happened to Mr. O'Brien?" Andrea asked.

"Died in a fire, years and years ago, when he was a young man. Not too long after they married."

"Did they have children?" Andrea figured she might as well make conversation, even though she knew Vivian had no survivors.

A small, child-like smile appeared briefly on Mrs. Newsome's face. "Well ... maybe," she said.

"Maybe?"

The old woman reached up and moved her fingers from one side of her lips to the other, as if zipping them shut.

"Is it a secret?" Andrea asked, getting no response. Her heartbeat quickened. "Mrs. Newsome, this is very important to me. I ... " She hesitated only seconds before deciding to bend the truth. "I was sent here by Vivian's family ... to see if I could bring them all together again."

Mrs. Newsome's zippered lips relaxed once again into a soft smile. "Oh," she said. "Oh, my, how nice."

"Vivian's children?" Andrea probed.

"Just one." She leaned closer and whispered, "Out of wedlock." Andrea whispered back, "I see."

"Couple o' years *after* Mr. O'Brien died." Her eyes were bright with the knowledge of a long-kept secret. She ran her tongue across her dry, crackly lips a few times, then she was ready to tell the tale.

"No one knew. Just me. She told me 'bout a year or so before she died. She knew I could keep a secret."

"You've done very well," Andrea assured her. She waited.

"Came to visit, the child did, all grown up. One visit. Many, many years ago. Never saw Vivian so happy before or since."

"What was the child's name?"

Mrs. Newsome yawned unashamedly, mouth wide open. "Don't remember. I'm getting tired."

"Was it a daughter or son?"

"A girl." She brightened a little. "Vivian didn't have her baby here in this town. No, ma'am. Went to her aunt, she did. In Birmingham."

A chill flew up Andrea's spine. "Birmingham?" she asked, not sure she had heard correctly.

Mrs. Newsome nodded, then rang the bell for assistance. "Birmingham, Alabama," she said. "To her Aunt Mary."

The words hit like a bolt of lightning.

Chapter 23

"I think it's time to visit your Aunt Mary in Birmingham," Alex said that evening. They were sitting on the big, plush sofa in the den.

"It's a coincidence, Alex, it has to be. If Evelette did have an Aunt Mary—and I'm not sure she did—the woman would have to have been born at least 120 years ago. My Aunt Mary is an *infant* compared to that!"

"Of course it's not the same person. I'm only saying that the answer lies in Birmingham."

"Besides," Andrea went on, finishing her thought, "Jenny was an only child. And there was never any mention in the diaries of her parents having brothers or sisters in this country. No woman named Mary was ever mentioned. Not once."

"Darling, you're getting a little mixed up." He pulled her closer, pressing her head to his shoulder. "If Evelette were raised by the Doyles, her Aunt Mary would be one of *their* family, not an Alcott.

Andrea sighed. "You're right," she said. "I've been at this far too long. I'm losing my grip. But ... I'm afraid there won't be any peace for me until I understand what's going on."

"I know."

"I have got to find out why I feel so ... so embroiled in all of this. I told you about the effect the house had on me the first time I saw it—during the Christmas tour. And every time since then, when I've

197

gone near that four-poster bed, I've felt as if it were trying to tell me something. It's weird, Alex. Maybe Violet was right when she left the bed in the house, thinking that the spirit of the real Jenny would remain. … Then there's that damn fluttering curtain business."

"What fluttering curtain business?"

Andrea looked at him with a bit of a twinkle in her eye. "I never mentioned it because I was afraid you'd think I was crazier than you *already* think I am." She laughed at herself, and told him, "It's happened, oh, maybe eight or ten times since we moved in. I'll be alone in one of the rooms and a curtain will move at one of the windows. Except the window isn't open and there's no breeze."

"Hmmm."

"Most often, it happens when I touch Jenny's bed." She laughed again, this time at the expression on his face. Then she got serious. "Think about it for just a minute, Alex. What if Jenny's spirit *is* in this house? What if she's trying to tell me something by making the curtains move? Or maybe she's trying to encourage me. Maybe she *wants* me to find Evelette!"

"Well," Alex said. He really didn't believe any of it. Not for a minute. But he loved his wife. "I've always heard that in order for a spirit to speak to a living person, the person has to be receptive to the spirit. I'd say you're definitely receptive to Jenny's spirit. When you arrived here, you were able to cross the dimension of time, because you and Jenny were—are—kindred spirits. You both have experienced the loss of a child, grief, guilt and uncertainty. I'm sure that in the end she was uncertain about the path she had chosen for her life, which compounds the fact that she had to take her grief and guilt with her to her grave."

Andrea was quiet for a moment, then said, "Maybe I'm not the one who needs to find peace. Maybe it's Jenny."

He gave her another hug. "Like I said, let's go to Birmingham."

"Let's? You mean you would go with me?"

"Even lawyers take vacations."

"You just spent a week in New York."

"That was not a vacation. *This* will be a vacation."

~~~

But Alex couldn't go to Birmingham that week or the next. Business was picking up and he still had no one he could trust to leave in charge. His one employee, who had kept the office open while he'd been in New York, had bollixed the accounting system, and that had to be put in order again.

Andrea stayed fidgety for two days. That was all the longer she could wait before doing something. It was then that she remembered the line in the obituary, which read, "Burial will be in Spring Hill Cemetery." She would go there, wherever it was. She would find the grave. It probably wouldn't be forthcoming with information, but at least she wouldn't be at home pacing the floor!

"Where, exactly, is Spring Hill Cemetery?" she asked her neighbor, Mr. Pinckney, across the fence.

"Right beside Spring Hill Church," he replied.

Andrea waited while he smiled at his own little joke.

"The church is about ten or so miles out Spring Hill Road," he said.

She smiled a little, too. "Which is?"

"About half a mile from the bypass on the south end of town."

She left immediately.

~~~

Andrea didn't know what to expect at Spring Hill, certainly not what she found. The little white clapboard church—very, very old— sat back in the trees, listing slightly to the right on its foundation. The porch, obviously built in recent years, was straight as an arrow, lending the structure the charm of imperfection. Off to the right was an arbor, also of recent years, probably for "dinner on the grounds." Back of the church, the inevitable outhouse.

Andrea went up the church steps and peeked in the window. The sun was shining brightly into the one-room sanctuary from the left side, and she could see clearly the straight-backed wooden pews, the wood slab floor, the small altar, the raised pulpit, the ancient upright piano and the "air-conditioning"—fans, probably donated by a funeral home. She could easily picture the child, Evelette, attending church here with her adopted family. She also could see Evelette, the woman, arranging flowers on the little table in front of the pulpit, or playing the piano.

If Evelette is buried here, it must have been true that Becca gave the baby to a family who lived nearby, she thought. *They must never have used her given name, or surely Evelyn, if not Jenny, would have found her.*

She descended the steps and walked to the small graveyard at the left of the church. The headstones were old and weathered, some chipped, though the cemetery had had excellent care. Grass was carefully mowed, and here and there a bouquet of flowers brightened a grave. She moved slowly, reading epitaphs: "Old soldier, rest here, ye'r days of war are o'er." And "Gone forever, forgotten never." Sadly, there were several infant graves.

Finally, toward the back under the shade of a cluster of oak trees, she found a grouping of Doyles: Martin and Hazel, with "infant son"; George and Phyllis; Dean ("Alone for all his days on earth, alone no more"); and Harold and Annabelle. Next to Annabelle were two headstones: Charles Michael O'Brien, husband; and his wife, Vivian Anna Evelette Doyle O'Brien.

Tears began streaming down Andrea's face.

~~~

"At least now I know we have the right person," she said to Alex. She had gone to his office on Jackson Street. She couldn't wait until he came home to give him the news.

"And we know she spent time in Birmingham," he said. He waited. He knew her well enough to know exactly where her mind would go next.

"Her child! She went there to have a child! Oh, Alex, what if we could put those diaries into her child's hands? Jenny's granddaughter would then know how much Jenny loved Evelette. She would know about her family, her origins."

"She could be right here in Thomasville."

"Or not. My guess is that the baby was adopted in Birmingham, because Mrs. Newsome at the nursing home at first said that Vivian had no children, remember? She made a big deal of its being a secret."

"You know it's going to be another week or two before I can go with you to Birmingham. Why don't you call your Aunt Mary and make arrangements to go see her right now. Just you."

"Alex—" She started to object, but he stopped her.

"You two women would have much more fun solving this mystery without me. Besides, I know you want to get going. You really don't want to wait."

That was certainly true. She stood there like a lump, eyes wide, not knowing what to say.

"And you'd better not feel *guilty* about leaving me here," he added with a smile. "I have plenty to occupy my mind."

She grinned, then squealed, then hugged him around the neck just as a client walked through the door. "Excuse me," she said to the client as she flew past him. "See you for dinner, Alex!"

"I'm taking you out!" he called.

"Yessss!" And she was out the door.

~~~

Andrea's Aunt Mary was still the most terrific person Andrea had ever known, and, at fifty-two, she was still beautiful, athletic and energetic. She and her husband, Fred Wells, lived in a comfortable brick home in a quiet subdivision. Fred was a chiropractor who had a clinic next to a luxury hotel. He said that was where most of his business came from!

"She went to her Aunt Mary in Birmingham? How spooky," said Mary after listening to the whole story.

"Isn't it, though? When I heard that, I felt ice go through my veins. Talk about *déjà vu!*"

"Well, where shall we start?" Mary asked.

"I can't even imagine," Andrea said. "There's no point in trying adoption records, because we're not even related to these people."

"And maybe Evelette's child—who would be, umm, lets's see … in her early eighties now—might not want to know all this. She may not even know she was adopted."

"But *I* need to know, and Jenny needs to know; otherwise, she'll never stop waving those curtains at me!"

Mary laughed—the same warm, musical sound that Andrea had found so comforting all those years ago. And once again she felt comforted. She knew she had come to the right place.

So they turned to the Internet on the computer in Mary's home office, looking for a birth record of any child born to Vivian O'Brien in Birmingham around 1919 or 1920. They tried a variety of websites under "ancestors" and "genealogy," finally turning up one with a listing of O'Briens, but it required a credit-card payment for further search. Andrea quickly punched in the numbers and hit *go!*

Scrolling through, they struck gold—Daughter to Vivian O'Brien, unwed, 1919.

Further search? Enter credit-card number for payment.

"Again?" Mary asked.

Andrea entered it quickly.

And there she was: Doris Anna O'Brien, born July 8, 1919.

Andrea sat back in her chair, her face white.

"I see it, too," Mary said after a moment. "Same first two names. Same birth date. She didn't grow up as O'Brien, though. Doris Anna Meade took the name of her adoptive parents."

"It's my mother."

~~~

Doris Anna: adopted by the Meades, married to the Coopers. Proving it—that Evelette's daughter was Andrea's mother—was fairly simple. Andrea contacted the Birmingham agency that had handled her mother's adoption, still in business after all these years.

Since the adoptee was deceased and Andrea could prove that she was Doris's birth daughter, she was given access to the records. It could not be more clear: Born to Vivian Anna Evelette Doyle O'Brien.

There was a note in the file, written by Evelette:

> *Dear Doris Anna,*
>
> *If you ever ask for your adoption records, I want you to have them. I want you to know that I have always loved you more than life itself. But I could not keep you. I am 69 years old now. My husband, Charlie O'Brien, went to heaven many years ago, and I barely had enough money to support myself. Times were most difficult on the farm in those days. I knew that you would have a much better life with two parents who loved you and had the funds to support you. The agency promised me that you would be placed with a loving family. I trust that was so. I only regret that it took 12 years to find such a family for you.*
>
> *I did not know until last month that I, too, was adopted. My mother, Annabelle Doyle, told me as she lay dying in her bed. That is when I learned that my given name was Evelette, and that I was born to Jenny Alcott. You would know her— your grandmother—as Alissa Jennings, the famous dancer. Mother told me that my birth mother loved me dearly but was forced to give me away because of her age. To honor Jenny Alcott—who died last year, and whom I never had the privilege to meet—I have left instructions that the name she gave me— Evelette—be included on my gravestone.*
>
> *Doris Anna, if you ever decide to look for me, I will welcome you with open arms. I will tell you as much as I know about your birth family.*
>
> *Please know this—I love you!*
> *Your Mother,*
> *Vivian Evelette O'Brien*
> *December 10, 1962*

Andrea put the paper back in the file. Mary had been looking over her shoulder. "That is incredible," Mary said, breathless.

"What is even more incredible is that my mother *knew* about all of this and never told me! She read this letter and didn't even care enough to keep it. According to Mrs. Newsome at the life-care center in Thomasville, she visited Evelette. *Once!*"

"It's not so hard to imagine that your mother didn't tell you, Andrea. How do you suppose Doris—given her religious indoctrination by the over-zealous Cooper family—would have reacted to learning that her own grandmother was Alissa Jennings, the famous dancer known for brazen onstage behavior?"

"You're right. She would have hidden it. But why did she visit Evelette only once in all those years? Why did she withhold her love?"

"Why wouldn't she? She withheld it from you."

Andrea shut her eyes against burning tears.

"Still, don't be too hard on her, Andrea. Remember, I told you many years ago that she was a very nice person before becoming a Cooper. I liked her, but I was considered a little 'brazen' myself. I was the Cooper who rebelled."

"I remember." Andrea gave her a hug. "The best thing to come of all this is the knowledge that I am Jenny's great-granddaughter. Jenny has known it all along, and that is why she was trying to get my attention."

She blinked back a tear. "When I go home this time," she said, "I truly will be going *home!*"

The Graveyard at Springhill Church

Chapter 24

When Andrea returned, Alex Ferris found himself reevaluating his position on paranormal happenings. He hadn't believed in *déjà vu*, or talking spirits, or fluttering curtains, but he'd humored Andrea because he loved her so very much. Now he wondered if Jenny really had spoken to Andrea in some way, to guide her to Evelette, to Doris, and back to herself. It sure was weird, no matter how he looked at it. Two things were certain—since Andrea had come home from Birmingham, she was a hundred percent better emotionally, and she had dug into her artistic ambitions with unsurpassed passion!

Within a month, the attic room had become Andrea's studio. A construction crew had come in and closed off the unfinished back room (the squirrels were gone). In the studio they patched the floor, and sanded and refinished the diagonally-cut wood walls. They diverted air-conditioning to it, installed good lighting, and cut a skylight into the ceiling. Supplies were carried up and shelved, and her easel was placed under the skylight next to the Palladian windows along the front wall. The ballet bar remained in place. It, too, was patched and refinished. Andrea chose a thick area rug to cover most of the floor. As a final touch, she purchased a bentwood rocker at a local antiques store and had Alex help her carry it up the stairs.

"I thought you didn't like to sit in these things," Alex said.

"I won't be sitting in it," she replied.

"Then why are we bringing it up here?"

"Because Violet sat in a bentwood rocker while Jenny practiced at the ballet bar. It's for her."

Alex had no comment about that. He put the rocker in place and gave Andrea a hug. "Now that your studio is ready, and now that you're forty years old—"

"I am? Ohmygosh! My birthday was three days ago!"

"You forgot it, and I didn't want to remind you since you were having so much fun with this hideaway, and trying to get the workers to finish. So, how would you like to celebrate?"

"Ummm. Let's order in."

"You're kidding, of course."

"No, I'm not. Let's order something wonderful and eat it in bed, and then we can just stay there. In bed, I mean."

Alex grinned. "Sounds like a plan to me." He started toward the phone they'd had installed near the easel, then stopped. "Oh, while you were in Birmingham, some new neighbors moved in across the street."

"Into the Half House?"

He nodded. "Frank and Jeanie Bergen. They're our age. Frank's an accountant and Jeanie's a musician. They moved here from Augusta. You're going to like them. They said they were looking for some new 'best friends.'"

Andrea smiled as Alex picked up the phone to order dinner. She couldn't believe how happy she was! Everything was working out! She had found her family, rid herself of grief and guilt, and was finally chasing her artistic dreams. All because of a discovery in the attic, which led to another time, which led to saving herself and revitalizing her marriage … just in time.

~~~

The next morning, after Alex left for the office, Andrea went upstairs to the little front bedroom that had been Jenny's. The four-poster with the pineapple post-tops had been returned there, where it belonged. Violet's wedding handkerchief, framed and preserved behind glass, hung between the two front windows. The diaries were on the nightstand, and the sepia-tinted photo of a smiling young Jenny Alcott rested comfortably on the dresser in the beautiful silver frame that Alex had brought home from New York. Alex ... how she loved him!

Andrea sat down on the bed and began talking softly. "Jenny ... it's me, Andrea. I found Evelette. She had a daughter named Doris Anna. Guess what, Jenny—I am Doris Anna's daughter, your Evelette's granddaughter ... I am your great-granddaughter, Jenny. And I've come home."

Though the windows were closed and there was no breeze, one of the curtains fluttered ... then was still.

Becca's Apple Pie
(Makes 2 pies)

Filling:
Pare and slice a dozen or so big apples. Mix with 4 cups white sugar, a spoonful of cinnamon, a little nutmeg, some salt, and the juice of 2 thin-skinned lemons. Leave it alone while you make the crust.

Crust:
Mix up 4 cups flour, a little sugar and some salt. Add 2 cups lard (not full) and stir real good with a fork. Crack an egg into a cup and add 6 half-eggshells water and a spoonful of cider vinegar. Pour this into the flour to make dough.

Line tins with crust and dip filling into them. Put butter (size of a pecan) in the middle of each pie and add top crust. Bake.

Andrea's Version

<u>Filling (for one pie)</u>:

7 cups thinly sliced MacIntosh apples   2 cups sugar

2 Tablespoons lemon juice   teaspoon nutmeg

2 Tablespoons all purpose flour   ½ teaspoon cinnamon

¼ teaspoon salt   2 Tablespoons margarine

Combine lemon juice with apples. Mix dry ingredients together and pour over the apples. Stir and let stand while rolling out the crust. Pour filling into crust, using margarine to dot the top of the apple mixture; vent the top crust with a few good cuts and bake at 350º for one hour and 15 minutes.

<u>Crust (for two, 2-crust pies—one for now, and one to freeze in patties)</u>:

4 cups self-rising flour   1 Tablespoon sugar

½ teaspoon salt   1¾ cups vegetable shortening

Mix the above ingredients with fork or pastry blender. (Mix well.)

1 egg

½ cup water

1 Tablespoon vinegar

In a separate dish, beat the above three ingredients together with a fork. Combine the two mixtures until all moistened. Mold into a ball. Chill 15 minutes before lining the pie plates.